The Barrister's Binding

A Society of Polite Magic Novel

L. M. Valoris

PRODUCERS PUBLISHING

Title: *The Barrister's Binding*
Series: A *Society of Polite Magic Novel*

Published by Producers Publishing
www.producerspublishing.com

Edition & Identifiers

First paperback edition: **2026**
ISBN (Paperback): **978-1-969986-12-3**
eBook edition: **2026**

Contents

Chapter 1: The Null-Ink and the Ordinary Morning

The landlord's contract was a masterpiece of predatory architecture, and I was about to demolish it with a fountain pen.

The radiator clanked, indifferent to Tariq Ahmed's future hanging on a clause buried in paragraph seven. Working-class werewolves made easy targets; this landlord had drafted his terms with the cruelty of a man who enjoys fine print.

Debt-binding clause, third subsection, hidden behind standard late payment penalties.

The words swam in October light filtering through my office window. I removed my spectacles, pinched the bridge of my nose, replaced them. Plain wire frames from a mundane optician in Camden. Clear glass lenses.

My eyes, without the camouflage, glowed faint gold when I looked at magical contracts.

Better that my clients saw only a tired solicitor with ink-stained fingers and a cramped office in Clerkenwell. Better that they never understood exactly what I did for them.

I dressed the part: a high-collared blouse, a dark skirt, and a fitted jacket that could have belonged to a century ago.

I uncapped the Victorian fountain pen. The sterling silver had tarnished to pewter grey, the fine nib surviving a century of less delicate hands than mine. Mr. Grimsby had given it to me on my twenty-third birthday, three months before he died. Before he was murdered, though I'd never proven it and the Metropolitan Occult Police had declined to investigate thoroughly.

The ink, however, was my own innovation. A Null's only natural advantage, weaponised. I'd been born without a single thread attached to my soul—no magical signature, no binding potential, nothing for contracts or wards or compulsions to grip. To the magical world, I was a gap in the architecture. Invisible to enchantments. Immune to coercion. Useless, according to most practitioners, because what good was a Scribe who existed outside the very system she was meant to serve?

Considerable good, as it turned out. My Null essence, distilled into ink through a process Grimsby had called reckless and I called necessary, could introduce that same invisible quality into any contract it touched. Where my ink signed, bindings weakened. Threads frayed. The system's grip loosened, just enough to give someone like Tariq a fighting chance.

I touched the nib to the contract's witness line and signed my name. *Imogen Blackwell, Certified Scribe.* My left hand anchored the paper flat. The pen moved with controlled pressure, each letter formed exactly as the hundreds before it. When I finished, I set the pen down parallel to the contract's edge.

Then I removed my spectacles and looked.

Blue threads materialized across the paper, glowing against the grey morning. Each thread represented a binding, a magical connection between signatory and obligation. Most were solid and bright, indicating strong enforcement. The landlord's signature blazed rust-coloured at the bottom, earth magic marking his bloodline. Tariq's signature showed as silver, shifter magic stretched dangerously thin.

And where my signature sat, the threads frayed.

I traced the air above the paper, not quite touching it, following the line where my Null-Ink had done its work. The blue threads thinned and crossed at wrong angles, deliberately weakened. The clause that should have bound Tariq to fifteen years of debt servitude now hung by gossamer strands that would snap the first time he challenged them in Tribunal.

Fifteen years. And not just labour—the clause had been engineered to siphon Tariq's magical essence alongside his wages. Soul Equity, the old families called it, as if naming the theft made it civilised.

A werewolf's shifting power, drained incrementally through contract mechanics until nothing remained but a man who couldn't afford to be what he was born to be. This landlord had been feeding on Tariq's silver threads for months. I could see the thinning where the extraction had already begun.

The knot in my shoulder released. It was a tidy piece of work.

I blinked. The gold faded from my eyes. The threads vanished. The contract became merely paper again, covered in dense legal text that no one would read carefully except another Scribe.

Tariq sat across from me, knees pressed together, hands clasped white-knuckled. He was trying very hard not to look like someone who might shift in panic.

"That's it?" he asked quietly. "It's done?"

"It's done. The clause won't hold under challenge. If he tries to enforce it, you take it to Tribunal and the threads will fail when examined."

Tariq let out a breath that shook. "How much do I owe you?"

I slid the contract into my file stack. "What can you afford?"

His eyes flicked up, startled. "You—you did all that and you're still—"

"I'm not running a charity. But I'm not going to demand money you don't have."

Tariq's shoulders sagged. He reached into his jacket and produced a folded wad of notes. Not much. He offered them with both hands.

I accepted without ceremony and placed the money in my desk drawer. "If your landlord threatens you again, come back. Don't sign anything else without bringing it to me first."

He nodded rapidly, standing awkwardly with the contract copy I'd given him. "Thank you, Miss Blackwell."

"You're welcome. Now get out before you ask questions you don't want answered."

Tariq blinked, gave a grateful, confused half-smile, and left.

I watched the door close behind him and tried not to think about what happened next. Tariq would take that weakened contract to Tribunal. He would stand before an adjudicator and present the evidence I'd prepared. And he would do it alone, because my Scribe certification covered contract review and client consultation—solicitor's work. Arguing cases before the Tribunal required advocacy rights, which required examinations I couldn't afford and sponsorship from practitioners who would sooner see me struck off than elevated.

Grimsby had held full advocacy certification. He'd argued before the High Council itself, back when the Council still permitted challenges from outside the pureblood firms. He'd planned to sponsor my application the year he died.

I filed Tariq's contract and pulled the next case from my stack. The desk was where I belonged. The courtroom was for people with connections and credentials and the right kind of name. I almost believed that.

The office door swung open. "Imogen, I brought tea." Clara carried a ceramic pot painted with tiny flowers, her strawberry blonde hair escaping its pins. "And before you say anything, I reorganised the 2019 files because they were giving off terrible energy next to the 2020 ones."

Clara Vance. My flatmate, my office assistant, my—I didn't have a word for what Clara was. She'd arrived two years ago, fleeing a marriage that had left scars I pretended not to see. She'd stayed because I let her, and I let her because her presence made the office feel less like a bunker.

Supernatural London would have called her a hedge witch—a polite term for someone whose magic had been damaged beyond full recovery. The old pureblood families who governed through the High Council and kept order through the Metropolitan Occult Police had categories for everyone: pureblood, half-blood, hedge practitioner, shifter, fae, mundane-born. Neat labels that determined where you lived, what you earned, and how thoroughly the system could exploit you. Contracts were the mechanism. The Codex—supernatural London's labyrinth of binding law—was the weapon. And Scribes like me were supposed to serve that architecture, not pick it apart with fountain pens and stubbornness. Clara didn't fit their categories either. Perhaps that was why she'd stayed.

"You reorganised legal files by energy," I said.

"By *resonance*." She set the teapot down, nudging papers aside. "It's intuitive organization. The files feel better now."

A soft scratching came from atop the filing cabinet.

"If you've disturbed my system again," said a small, irritated voice, "I will file a formal complaint with the Registry."

Pip climbed down from his perch, all fourteen inches of indignant brownie in a too-large waistcoat. His amber eyes glowed faintly as he surveyed the damage Clara had done to his careful alphabetization.

"The Henderson file is now between Garcia and Morrison," he announced. "This is chaos. This is anarchy."

"It's where it wanted to be," Clara said serenely.

Pip made a sound of profound suffering and hopped onto my desk, examining the contract I'd just signed. His nose wrinkled.

"Debt servitude clause. Very fashionable among landlords this season." His voice dropped lower.

"Your pen work is getting bolder. If the Ethics Committee ever examines your signatures closely—"

"They won't," I said. Too sharp. I forced neutrality back into my voice. "They won't. I'm careful."

Pip's ears flattened, but he didn't press. Careful was the only reason I was still alive. Careful, and angry, and too stubborn to stop fighting a system that had been designed, with exquisite legal precision, to ensure that people like Tariq never escaped and people like me never mattered.

The anger was old. Comfortable. I wore it the way I wore my work coat—close to the skin, invisible to clients, warming nothing but myself.

Clara poured tea into mismatched mugs, watching me with the quiet attention she thought I didn't notice. "You look tired."

"I always look tired."

"You look *extra* tired."

"I'm fine."

Clara's mouth tightened, but she didn't push. She handed me a mug, the ceramic warm against my palms. "I was thinking we could go to the market after work. There's a new vendor with enchanted soaps."

"I have files to review."

"You always have files."

A knock at the door interrupted whatever Clara was about to say next.

We both turned. Pip's ears went rigid.

The knock came again. Not a client's hesitant tap—this was a firm, official sound. The kind of knock that expected to be answered.

Clara moved toward the door, but I was already standing. "Stay here."

I crossed the office in four steps and opened the door.

The courier on the landing wore no livery I recognised. Dark hair, pale face, expression carefully blank. He held a single envelope in gloved hands. His long, severe coat and immaculate gloves looked like a uniform from an older London where messages arrived on paper and never without consequence.

"Imogen Blackwell." Not a question. A statement. He was looking past Clara directly at me. "This requires your immediate attention."

Clara took the card hesitantly, turning it over in her hands. Heavy cardstock, cream-coloured, with an embossed seal I recognised even at this distance. She carried it to me, holding it as though it might bite.

I took it from her. Our fingers didn't touch. She dropped it the last inch and stepped back.

The seal was wax, dark blue, pressed with a symbol I'd spent five years trying to avoid: the Metropolitan Occult Police crest.

I broke the seal with my thumb. The card resisted slightly, stiff with enchantment. Inside, the message was brief and written in flawless copperplate script:

Your presence is required at the Thorne residence, Mayfair. A matter of supernatural homicide demands Scribe consultation. Attendance is not optional under Article Seven of the Supernatural Justice Act.

Lord Nathaniel Frost, Chief Inspector

Metropolitan Occult Police

I read it twice. The words didn't change. I set the card down on my desk, centered. Removed my spectacles. Set them beside the card. Pressed my palms flat on the desk surface, feeling the cool wood grain under my fingers.

The card's edges began to curl.

Blackness spread from the corners inward, and smoke rose in a thin column. Clara gasped. Pip had gone absolutely still, frozen in the prey animal instinct that all brownies shared when genuine danger manifested.

The card burned from outside in, turning to ash in seconds. The ash held its rectangular shape for a moment, perfect and intact, before collapsing into grey powder.

The courier still stood in the doorway. He nodded once, satisfied, then turned and left without another word.

Clara shut the door slowly. She leaned against it, staring at the ash on my desk. Her voice came out unsteady. "Imogen. What was that?"

I didn't answer immediately. I was mentally inventorying the contents of my locked drawer. The

Null-Ink. The client files that could never see daylight. The M.O.P. knew my name, knew my office location, knew enough about my work to summon me under Article Seven, which granted them authority to compel Scribe consultation in murder investigations. They'd sent a formal courier with enchanted cardstock, which meant this wasn't a polite request.

Supernatural homicide.

Mayfair.

The Thorne residence.

I knew that name. Elias Thorne, newly married, pureblood family with connections to the High Council. If he was dead, and if the M.O.P. needed a Scribe, it meant the death involved contract magic or blood oaths. Something impossible had happened, and they needed someone who could see threads.

"Imogen," Clara said again, her voice higher now. "Please."

I stood. The chair scraped back. I was moving on muscle memory now, gathering papers I'd need, returning the contract to the locked drawer, retrieving my coat from the hook.

"Stay here," I said. "Both of you. Don't answer the door. Don't take any calls."

Clara's face had gone pale. "You're scaring me."

"Good." I shrugged into my coat, checking the pockets by habit. Spectacles. Pen. The small protections I carried everywhere. "Stay scared. Stay careful. I'll be back when I can."

Pip climbed onto my shoulder, his small weight familiar and steadying. His claws pricked through my blouse fabric.

"If you're not back by nightfall," Clara said, "I'm coming to find you."

I paused at the door. Looked back at her—standing in the middle of our cramped, shabby, safe little office with her arms wrapped around herself and fear bright in her eyes.

"If I'm not back by nightfall," I said quietly, "don't."

I didn't wait for her response. I stepped into the hallway and pulled the door shut behind me.

The stairs creaked under my feet. Through the building's front entrance into grey drizzle. The street smelled of lamb fat and cumin from the kebab shop below. A red bus rumbled past, spraying mist from the gutter.

London, doing what it always did in October: damp, grey, indifferent to individual catastrophe.

I turned toward the Tube station, pulled my coat tighter against the rain, and walked toward Mayfair. Toward a murder in a pureblood household. Toward Lord Nathaniel Frost, whose name carried weight in supernatural London—the Council's favoured enforcer, the man who kept wards stable and peace intact.

The man who had just reached into my sanctuary and demanded I walk into his world.

My carefully maintained anonymity had lasted five years. Five years of invisible sabotage, of helping the powerless while staying beneath the notice of those with power.

It had lasted until this morning.

Chapter 2: The Impossible Crime

Green Park station disgorged me onto Piccadilly in a press of tourists and office workers, all hunched against the drizzle. I buttoned my coat to the throat and walked west, into the quiet geometry of Mayfair. The coat was cut in the old Council style—nipped waist, standing collar—because Mayfair treated modernity as a vulgar rumor.

The streets changed within three blocks. Noise fell away first—that was the tell. In Clerkenwell, noise was free, unavoidable. Here, silence was a commodity purchased at extraordinary expense. The buildings grew taller, their cream facades darkened by rain into something between ivory and bone. Black iron railings guarded narrow staircases descending to basement kitchens I would never see.

I checked the address on the paper slip I'd copied before leaving. Thorne residence. Curzon Street.

My shoes clicked against the wet pavement. No one else walked these streets. Through windows I glimpsed chandeliers, oil paintings in gilt frames, the kind of wealth that didn't need to announce itself because everyone already knew.

The wards appeared two blocks ahead.

Blue-silver ribbons stretched across the street at chest height, shimmering faintly in the grey light. Wards—the architecture of permission, magical barriers that decided who belonged somewhere and who didn't. Every building in supernatural London had them. But crime scene wards were different: designed not just to exclude, but to identify, contain, and if necessary, kill. The air tasted of ozone and static, pressure building behind my eyes. I stopped ten feet from the barrier.

Two M.O.P. constables stood at either end of the ward line, dark navy uniforms bearing silver insignia. The younger one noticed me first and approached with one hand raised. Their high collars and stiff tailoring belonged to another era, as if the M.O.P. had standardised on tradition and never updated the pattern.

"This is a restricted area, miss. You'll need to use the alternate route."

I showed him the paper slip. "Imogen Blackwell. Inspector Frost requested my presence."

He consulted a clipboard, found my name, and nodded without enthusiasm. "Through the barrier, straight ahead to number forty-seven. Don't touch anything."

I stepped toward the ward line. The pressure grew worse, vibrating through my ribs like standing too close to a massive bell.

I pushed through.

Cold honey. That's what it felt like. Resistance without substance, wrongness without pain. My Null status meant the wards couldn't bind me or turn me away, but they could still make their presence known—like a crowd parting reluctantly around someone they didn't want to acknowledge.

I emerged with my teeth aching and my skin crawling. The constable didn't react. To him, I'd simply walked through empty air.

Number forty-seven stood twenty meters ahead. White stone steps, black door standing open. Gas lamps glowed in the windows despite the morning light, flames enchanted to burn without fuel.

I climbed the steps and crossed the threshold.

The foyer made my office look like a storage cupboard. Marble floor in white and black diamonds, ceiling twelve feet high with ornate plasterwork. A grand staircase curved upward, its banister polished mahogany. The space smelled of beeswax polish and cold ash.

A man stood at the base of the staircase, writing in a leather notebook.

Tall—six feet two at least—with black hair silvering at the temples and a face built of sharp angles and aristocratic bone structure. His charcoal three-piece suit showed not a single crease, and a silver M.O.P. badge hung from a chain at his waist. The waistcoat fastened high beneath a starched collar and dark cravat, formal enough to pass for court wear in any century. He finished his line, dotted a punctuation mark with deliberate care, then closed the book with a sound that was both soft and final.

Only then did he turn to face me.

He approached with measured steps, stopping precisely six feet away—close enough to command attention, far enough to maintain hierarchy. Pale grey eyes moved over me with methodical attention, cataloguing clothing, posture, hands.

"Miss Blackwell." Not a question. "I am Lord Nathaniel Frost, Chief Inspector of the Metropolitan Occult Police Homicide Division."

"Inspector." I met his gaze, refusing to look down first.

"Your credentials."

"Scribe certification through the Inns of Court, registered five years ago under Marcus Grimsby. Independent practise in Clerkenwell specializing in contract review."

"Client base?"

"Mostly lower-income magical citizens. Werewolves, small covens, minor fae. Those who can't afford Council-approved counsel."

His expression flickered—something between disdain and irritation, quickly controlled. "Experience with homicide investigations?"

"No."

He waited. When I didn't elaborate, his jaw tightened almost imperceptibly.

"Follow me."

He turned without waiting, moving down the hallway toward the back of the house. His steps were silent on the marble—a man accustomed to moving through spaces that belonged to him regardless of ownership.

I followed, because I didn't have the luxury of refusing.

The hallway stretched long and wide, lined with paintings in gilt frames. Long-dead Thornes watched us pass. A grandfather clock ticked softly, its sound amplified by the silence.

Frost stopped at double doors guarded by two officers. The woman was in her forties with stern features and greying hair pulled tight—Sergeant insignia on her collar. The man was younger, stocky, with broad shoulders and a square jaw.

"Sergeant Halloway. Constable Duan. This is Miss Blackwell."

Halloway's eyes narrowed. "A civilian?"

"A Certified Scribe," Frost corrected, tone sharp enough to slice. "She will be assisting."

Assisting. The word landed with precision. Not investigating, not advocating, not representing anyone's interests. Assisting. The way a clerk assisted a solicitor, or a solicitor assisted a barrister—always the subordinate verb, always someone else's authority borrowed and never owned. My Scribe certification gave me the right to review contracts and advise clients. It did not give me standing to examine evidence, question witnesses, or make arguments in formal proceedings. In this house, in this investigation, I was a pair of specialised eyes attached to an inconvenient opinion.

Frost knew it. Halloway knew it. And they expected me to know it too.

He opened the doors. The parlor smelled like death. Not rot—too fresh—but something metallic and wrong, like blood diluted in expensive perfume. The air was cold, colder than the foyer, as though the wards had tightened their grip.

I paused at the threshold. The doorframe held a faint shimmer, ward-work layered in quiet complexity. Someone had sealed the room from the inside out, like a lid placed over a pot to keep something contained.

Frost watched me pause. "Problem?"

"Observation."

"Observe quickly."

I stepped into the parlor.

Large room, richly furnished in cream and gold. Heavy curtains drawn over bay windows. A chandelier caught light that didn't exist. Fireplace unused, cold ash in the grate. Two sofas, several chairs, a polished coffee table with a silver tray holding a decanter and two untouched glasses.

A body lay in the center of the room on a Persian rug.

Halloway stood near the fireplace taking photographs. Another officer—younger, Asian heritage, forensic division markings—crouched beside the body with a notebook and latex gloves.

I stopped three feet from the corpse.

Late twenties. Blonde hair, pale skin. Evening clothes that cost more than my entire wardrobe. No visible wounds. Eyes closed. Arms at his sides in a position too perfect to be accidental.

"Name?" I asked, though I already suspected.

"Elias Thorne," Frost said. "Eldest son of Lord and Lady Thorne. Found at six thirty this morning by household staff. No signs of forced entry. No signs of struggle. No mundane cause of death."

"No cause of death at all," the forensic officer added quietly. "Heart intact. No hemorrhaging. No toxins detected. No bruising."

"Yet he's dead," Halloway said flatly, snapping another photograph. "So something happened."

Frost's eyes remained on me. "This is where you come in."

I glanced at the rug beneath Elias Thorne. The pattern was intricate, but something about it made my skin itch. Not the fabric—the air. The wards. The way the room held itself too still, like a held breath.

"What exactly are you asking me to do?"

"Use your abilities. Determine whether magic was involved. If so, what kind."

"And if I determine it was?"

"Then you tell me." His tone suggested the answer was obvious. "We are investigating multiple deaths of similar nature. All within Council jurisdiction. All with no visible cause. The Council has requested my division's involvement. They have also requested a Scribe."

"You requested me," I corrected.

His gaze sharpened. "Yes."

"Why?"

"Because your name appeared on a contract in the victim's possession."

My pulse stuttered. "A contract."

The forensic officer stood, removing her gloves. "We found a lease agreement in Elias Thorne's desk drawer. Signed by him. Signed by an unidentified tenant. Witnessed by you."

Of course. Of course my work would circle back like a curse.

"What kind of lease?"

"A property in Clerkenwell. Building owned by the Thorne family. The tenant was a werewolf named Tariq Ahmed."

My stomach dropped. Tariq. The contract I'd sabotaged yesterday.

Frost watched my face with surgical precision. He saw the flicker of recognition. He saw the moment my composure cracked and welded itself back together.

"Your client?"

"Yes." The word tasted like ash.

"Then you will assist us. Because your work intersects with this investigation. Because someone killed Elias Thorne and left your name in his papers. Because the Council is concerned about wealthy magical citizens dying in ways that might attract mundane attention. And because if you refuse, you will make yourself suspicious."

Halloway snorted. "She's already suspicious."

Frost's eyes didn't leave mine. "Miss Blackwell, I am not in the habit of making requests. I make directives."

"And I am not in the habit of working under M.O.P. supervision."

Something shifted in his posture. A subtle realignment, like a chess piece moved into place. His politeness was a veneer; beneath it, power waited, cold and absolute.

"You will work under Metropolitan Occult Police authority," he said evenly, "or you will not work at all."

My fingers curled inside my gloves. "Is that a threat?"

"It is a statement of jurisdiction. You are within an active ward perimeter. You are in a Council-class crime scene. You have been summoned. You do not have the right to refuse."

"Two courts," I murmured before I could stop myself.

Frost's eyes narrowed. "What was that?"

"Nothing."

Halloway's mouth twitched as if she wanted to smile and didn't allow herself.

"You will review the prior cases at Blackfriars Citadel after we complete initial scene processing," Frost said. "You will provide analysis. You will assist. If you attempt to leave, you will be detained."

The word *detained* was mundane. The implication was not.

"Fine," I said. "I'll assist."

Frost inclined his head—a small acknowledgment of victory. "Good decision."

"We'll need her statement," Halloway said. "And we should check that lease for irregularities."

My stomach tightened. "The lease is standard."

A lie. Frost noted it without calling me on it.

"Then we will examine it," he said.

Of course he would.

I moved to the side, watching officers work while I waited for my turn with the body. Their movements were efficient, practised. Mundane procedure applied to supernatural crime.

Finally, Frost gestured toward Elias Thorne. "Now. Examine."

I removed my spectacles and held them in my left hand. Closed my eyes for three seconds to shift my vision. Opened them again.

The world stripped down to its architecture.

The rug vanished into transparency. The floorboards became geometry. And rising from the sternum of Elias Thorne, two thick golden cords emerged.

No. *Ended.* Ragged golden threads hung from his chest, thick as rope, frayed at their termination points. The ends were blackened. Scorched. The magical equivalent of cauterization, as if whatever had cut these cords had burned while doing so.

Marriage bonds. Soul-linked. The kind of oath that couldn't be broken while both parties lived because the magic was self-enforcing, drawing power from life force itself.

Someone had severed them.

I reached toward the threads without touching, my hand hovering inches above his chest. The air felt wrong. Colder than the rest of the room.

"Explain what you're seeing." Frost's voice, clinical.

I kept my gaze on the threads. Easier to speak to them than to him. "Two marriage bonds. Thick gauge, indicating significant magical investment. Gold colouring confirms soul-binding rather than simple legal contract. The bonds have been severed cleanly, approximately six inches from their anchor point."

Too clean—no recoil filaments, no secondary thread-lash, as if the severance had been done in a vacuum.

"Can marriage bonds be severed?" Halloway asked.

"They can be dissolved. Through mutual agreement. Through certain Tribunal proceedings. Through death."

"Yet they are severed," Frost said.

"Yes. Which means someone did something that should be impossible."

"Impossible is not a word I accept. What mechanism?"

I examined the burn marks. "Not spell-work. Magic leaves different residues. This suggests physical cutting. An object. Something sharp enough to slice through magical constructs as if they were material."

The forensic officer spoke from behind me. "Inspector, a binding curse on the victim's ghost would support deliberate planning. Someone who could silence the dead would have access to rare artifacts."

Halloway swore under her breath. "So we're dealing with someone who can kill without leaving a mark, cut marriage bonds, and bind ghosts. Wonderful."

Frost's gaze flicked to me. "Can you confirm the binding?"

I turned my Thread Sight outward. Normally, death left a shimmer—threads unraveling, magical residue clinging to surfaces. Here, the air was unnaturally clean. The wards held everything in place.

It felt staged.

"There should be more," I said. "There isn't."

Frost's eyes sharpened. He liked confirmation.

I stood, replacing my spectacles. My eyes stopped glowing, but I felt exposed. Frost had watched me use abilities most people never witnessed.

"Any indication of who severed the bonds?"

"No. The cut is too clean. Whoever did this knew exactly what they were doing."

"Or had something that did," Halloway muttered.

"The marriage bonds belonged to whom?" Frost asked.

"Elias Thorne and his spouse. If he was married."

"He was. To Lady Seraphina Thorne."

My chest constricted. The name carried weight—old money, old magic, rumored Council connections.

"Where is she?"

Frost's gaze was flat. "Missing."

"Gone since last night," Halloway said. "Household staff claim she went to bed at eleven. She wasn't there this morning. No one saw her leave."

"So either she's our killer or our next victim."

Frost's eyes stayed on me. "This is why we need you."

My hands were cold inside my gloves. "You said multiple deaths."

"Three. All wealthy. All within Council jurisdiction. All with severed bonds. All with bound ghosts."

"Two courts," I repeated, quieter this time.

Frost heard it. This time he didn't ask.

We stood in silence for a moment—me, him, the body between us, the officers moving through their procedures. Then he turned away.

"Finish processing. Miss Blackwell stays close."

I watched him walk toward the window, his reflection sharp against the grey light. He didn't look back, but I felt his attention remain on me like a weight.

I looked down at Elias Thorne again. At the perfect stillness. At the severed bonds that should not have been severed.

Evidence that felt too neat was evidence that had been arranged.

And my name was in his desk. My client was in his records. My work—my careful, invisible, illegal work—was suddenly visible to the one institution I'd spent five years avoiding.

Manners were protocol. Protocol was power.

And Frost had just shown me exactly how much of it he wielded.

Chapter 3: The Pattern and the Warrens

I arrived at Blackfriars Citadel at nine the following morning with Clara's voice still echoing in my skull.

He can't force you to do this. There are laws. Protections.

I'd explained, as patiently as exhaustion allowed, that those protections existed at the pleasure of the High Council, and Lord Nathaniel Frost had made it clear whose authority would prevail. Pip had been less optimistic, muttering about aristocratic bastards and inevitable betrayals while reorganizing case files with violent efficiency. Neither of them had slept. Neither had I.

The Citadel rose from the Thames embankment like a concrete tumor—seven stories of windowless authority, save for narrow slits designed for archers rather than natural light. Iron gates flanked stone pillars carved with ward sigils I recognised from textbooks but had never seen deployed at this scale. The architecture made no pretense of welcome. Every line, every shadow, every deliberate absence of ornament communicated the same message: power resided here, and those who entered did so at its pleasure.

I held my document case like a shield and walked toward the entrance.

The suppression field settled over me at the threshold like a heavy wool coat in summer—stifling, pressure-inducing, impossible to shed. Ward-work always caused physical sensation, even for Nulls. But this wasn't the honey-resistance of a private home or the brief pressure of a commercial barrier. This was active suppression, deliberate, as if someone had wrapped chains around every magical particle in the air and pulled tight.

My stomach lurched. I kept walking.

The entrance hall was granite and iron, designed to make visitors feel small. A desk sergeant examined my credentials with the enthusiasm of someone reviewing sewage reports, then directed me to the third floor. Interview Room Seven.

The corridors were narrow, the lighting inadequate, the air thick with old magic and institutional indifference. Officers passed without acknowledgment. I climbed stairs that seemed designed to exhaust petitioners before they reached anyone important.

Frost waited outside Interview Room Seven, checking his pocket watch. He closed it with a sharp snap when he saw me approach.

"Miss Blackwell. Punctual."

"Inspector."

He opened the door and gestured me inside.

The room was small, windowless, iron filigree worked into the stone walls in patterns that made my eyes want to skip over them. A metal table bolted to the floor held three case folders, a carafe of water, and two glasses no one had touched. Two chairs faced each other across the table. The lighting came from mage-globes that cast everything in flat, shadowless illumination.

Frost took the chair facing the door. I took the other, setting my document case on the floor beside me.

"Before we proceed to the Southwark location," he said, "you will review the prior cases. Full context is necessary for effective analysis."

He slid the first folder across the table.

I opened it. Crime scene photographs. Autopsy reports. Contract documentation. A man's face stared up at me from the top photograph—young, handsome, with the slight blandness of inherited wealth.

"Marcus Bellingham," Frost said. "Aged thirty-two. Married eight months to Helena Ashworth, daughter of Lord Ashworth. Found in his Kensington townhouse by his valet. Cause of death: catastrophic magical feedback from severed marriage bond threads. No forced entry. No signs of struggle. Wards intact."

I turned pages. The Thread Sight analysis had been performed by someone competent—the diagrams showed the same blackened termination points I'd seen on Elias Thorne's bonds. Clean cuts. Surgical precision.

"The spouse?"

"Alive. Traumatized by the bond severance but physically unharmed. She remembers nothing of the night in question. Memory glamour, according to our specialists."

I set the folder aside. Frost slid the second across.

"Edmund Cartwright. Aged twenty-nine. Married six months to Isabelle Montague. Found in his Chelsea residence by household staff. Identical cause of death. Identical lack of evidence."

The photographs showed another young man, another expensive home, another body positioned too perfectly on another Persian rug. The pattern was becoming clear—and disturbing.

"All newly married," I said. "All purebloods. All wealthy."

"All with marriage bonds representing significant magical investment," Frost added. "The Bellingham-Ashworth union merged two ancient bloodlines. The Cartwright-Montague marriage consolidated substantial property holdings. The Thorne match—"

"Let me guess. Also strategically valuable."

"Lady Seraphina brought connections to three Council families and access to a vault of pre-Reformation artifacts." Frost's voice remained clinical. "These were not love matches, Miss Blackwell. They were mergers. And someone is liquidating them."

I stared at the photographs. Three men, dead. Three wives, traumatized or missing. Three sets of marriage bonds severed by something that shouldn't exist.

"The pattern suggests the killer knows their schedules. Knows when they'll be alone."

"Or knows how to ensure they will be." Frost leaned back slightly. "The High Council is concerned."

"Concerned is an interesting word choice for panic."

His mouth didn't smile, but something flickered in his eyes. "The Council believes that if blood oaths can be broken, the entire social contract of supernatural London becomes unreliable. Contracts that should be unbreakable can be severed. Wards that should be permanent can be dissolved. The foundation of our legal and magical system fails."

"That assumes the method can be replicated."

"Which is why we must determine what method was used." Frost stood and walked to the wall, his back to me. "I need a Scribe's expertise. Whether through legal loopholes in the original contracts, through artifact use your Thread Sight can identify, or whether—" A pause. "A rogue Scribe has found a method to break bindings that should be absolute."

The implication landed like a blow.

"You think a Scribe is involved."

"I think it's a possibility the Council is taking seriously." He turned to face me. "One theory currently circulating is that a rogue Scribe has discovered a method to sever blood oaths—either through artifact use or through loopholes in contract law. If that theory gains traction, the Council will implement emergency measures."

"What kind of measures?"

"Audit every Scribe in London. Strip certifications. Eliminate anyone they deem suspicious." His grey eyes held mine. "Scribes are essential to supernatural society's legal framework. But you're also a small population. Vulnerable. Replaceable through training new practitioners if older ones are deemed compromised."

The warding stone in my pocket—the one he'd given me at the crime scene—grew heavier. Or perhaps that was my own grip tightening around nothing.

"You're telling me I'm not just investigating murders. I'm protecting every Scribe in London."

"I'm telling you the stakes extend beyond individual victims. If you find evidence of Scribe involvement, report it immediately. If you find evidence exonerating the profession, document it thoroughly. Either way, the Council needs answers before they implement solutions that cannot be reversed."

I closed the second folder and set it atop the first. Three dead men. Three broken bonds. One impossible method. And the entire Scribe profession hanging in the balance.

"What's in Southwark?"

Frost returned to the table and collected the folders with precise movements. "A secondary thread. Traced from the Thorne crime scene. It terminates at a location in the Warrens."

The Warrens. I'd heard the name—everyone in working-class supernatural London had. The network of tunnels and abandoned stations where the contract-broken gathered, where those who'd fled binding servitude or failed their magical obligations eked out existence in the spaces between worlds. The kind of place M.O.P. pretended didn't exist until it became convenient to raid.

"You traced a thread to the Warrens and you're bringing me?"

"The thread is fading. It requires Thread Sight to follow before it degrades entirely." He moved toward the door. "Sergeant Halloway and Officer Duan will accompany us. We leave in ten minutes."

"Inspector." He paused with his hand on the door. "Why me? You said my name appeared in Thorne's papers, but that's not sufficient reason to bring a potential suspect into active investigation."

Frost was silent for a moment. Then: "Because Marcus Grimsby trained you."

My breath caught.

"Grimsby was investigating systematic contract fraud before his death," Frost continued, not turning around. "Predatory lending practises, debt servitude schemes, exploitation of working-class supernatural beings by Council families. He died before he could present his findings to the High Council. The official report listed ward failure." He paused. "I was the investigating officer. I was ordered to close the case."

"By whom?"

"Parties with sufficient political influence to ensure compliance." His voice was flat. "I was younger then. More obedient to institutional authority. More willing to believe the system would correct itself."

"And now?"

"Now I have three bodies, an impossible murder weapon, and a pattern that suggests someone is eliminating threats to a system built on exploitation." He opened the door. "You're here because Grimsby trained you to see what others miss. Because you've spent five years helping the people that system was designed to crush. And because I believe you want justice for your mentor as much as I want answers for these victims."

He left without waiting for my response.

I sat alone in the interview room, surrounded by iron and stone and the weight of everything he'd just revealed. Grimsby. Murdered. Frost had known—had investigated—had been silenced.

And now he was reopening doors that powerful people had paid to keep closed.

I gathered my document case and followed him into the corridor.

The Warrens entrance hid in plain sight.

Southwark High Street bustled with midday traffic—mundanes flowing past the boarded-up Tube station without a second glance, their eyes sliding off the weathered timber like water off oil. The glamour was old, greasy, and effective. A hundred years of accumulated misdirection layered over the threshold until it became invisible to anyone not specifically looking.

I stood before the sealed entrance with Frost on my right and Pip perched on my left shoulder, one tiny hand gripping my collar for balance. He'd insisted on coming, despite my protests, and had spent the car ride glaring at Frost with undisguised suspicion from inside my document case.

Halloway and Duan flanked us at careful distance, hands near their equipment. The afternoon sun was pale, filtering through London's perpetual cloud cover.

"The thread continues inside," I said, Thread Sight active. The golden filament I'd traced from Elias Thorne's chest extended through the glamour and into darkness beyond. Fainter now than it had been yesterday, degrading with each passing hour. "We need to move before it fades completely."

Frost removed a warding stone from his pocket—smooth polished granite engraved with sigils that hurt to look at directly—and pressed it against the boards. The glamour didn't dissolve; it flinched. The timber rippled, then parted like a curtain, revealing a staircase descending into blue-green darkness.

"Standard formation," Frost said. "I take point. Sergeant Halloway, rear guard. Duan, document everything. Miss Blackwell stays close and does not engage any hostile elements."

"I'm not a child."

"You're a civilian asset in an unstable environment. If I tell you to withdraw, you withdraw. Understood?"

I understood that arguing would waste time we didn't have. "Understood."

We descended.

The stairs were Victorian-era construction, wrought iron and crumbling brick, designed for a Tube station that had never officially opened. The air grew colder with each step, carrying the scent of damp stone and something older—the distinct mustiness of spaces that existed between official records.

At the bottom, the tunnel opened into a cavern that shouldn't have fit beneath Southwark's streets. The ceiling arched thirty feet overhead, supported by pillars carved with symbols I didn't recognise. Blue-green mage-lights floated in irregular clusters, casting shadows that moved independently of any source.

People lived here.

I saw them in doorways and alcoves—huddled figures watching our descent with wary eyes. Makeshift shelters constructed from salvaged materials lined the tunnel walls. A small market had established itself near a junction, vendors selling items I couldn't identify from this distance.

The contract-broken. The debt-fled. The ones who'd slipped through the cracks of supernatural society and found refuge in its forgotten spaces.

"They won't interfere," Halloway said quietly. "M .O.P. has an understanding with the Warrens. We don't raid; they don't harbor violent criminals."

"An understanding," I repeated. "How civilized."

Frost shot me a look but said nothing.

The golden thread led deeper into the tunnel network, past the market, past the shelters, into passages that grew narrower and darker. Pip's claws dug into my shoulder as the ceiling lowered and the walls pressed closer.

"Miss Blackwell." Frost had stopped ahead, his mage-light illuminating a doorway carved into the tunnel wall. "The thread terminates here."

I moved to stand beside him, Thread Sight straining against the darkness. The golden filament passed through the doorway and ended abruptly six feet inside—not frayed like a broken connection, but severed. Cut clean, just like the bonds on Elias Thorne's chest.

"Someone was here," I said. "Someone connected to Thorne's marriage bond. But the connection's been cut."

"Can you determine when?"

"Within the last forty-eight hours. The residue hasn't fully degraded."

Frost stepped through the doorway. I followed, Pip's small body tense against my neck.

The room beyond was small, circular, carved from the living rock. Empty except for a stone plinth in the center—and the symbols covering every inch of the walls.

I recognised some of them. Contract sigils. Binding marks. The visual language of magical obligation rendered in what looked disturbingly like dried blood.

"This is a workshop," I breathed. "Someone's been practicing here. Experimenting with bond manipulation."

Duan had produced a camera and was photographing everything, her flash strobing against the symbols. Halloway stood guard at the doorway, one hand on her baton.

Frost crouched beside the plinth, examining something on its surface. "Miss Blackwell. Your assessment."

I moved closer, activating Thread Sight fully.

The plinth blazed with residual magic—layers of it, accumulated over months or years of use. Someone had been severing bonds here, systematically, repeatedly. The magical signature was complex, artifact-assisted, but I could see the underlying pattern.

"They're not just cutting bonds," I said slowly. "They're harvesting them. The severance isn't destruction—it's extraction. Someone is collecting the magical energy stored in marriage bonds."

"For what purpose?"

I traced the flow of residual threads, following them to their termination point. They converged on a symbol I didn't recognise—something that looked like a closed fist wrapped in chains.

"I don't know. But whatever they're building, they need a lot of power to do it. The kind of power stored in soul-linked bonds between ancient bloodlines."

Frost stood, his expression unreadable. "Document everything. I want this room analysed by specialists before we leave."

He moved toward the doorway, then paused. "Miss Blackwell. Your mentor was investigating systematic exploitation. Someone is now systematically harvesting from the families that built that system." He met my eyes. "Do you believe in coincidence?"

"No."

"Neither do I."

He left to coordinate with Halloway. I remained in the workshop, surrounded by blood-drawn symbols and the residue of impossible magic, and tried to make the pieces fit.

Grimsby had been investigating exploitation. He'd died before he could expose it. Now someone was killing the exploiters—but not for justice. For power. Harvesting their bonds like crops, storing energy for a purpose I couldn't yet see.

And somewhere in the middle of it all, my name sat in a dead man's desk, linking me to a web I hadn't known existed.

Pip's small voice came from my shoulder, barely above a whisper. "Miss Blackwell. We should leave this place."

"I know."

"I mean we should leave and never return. This magic is old. Wrong. The kind of wrong that doesn't wash off."

I looked at the symbol of the fist wrapped in chains. At the converging threads. At the careful, patient architecture of something being built in darkness.

"I don't think leaving is an option anymore, Pip."

His claws tightened on my collar. "No. I don't suppose it is."

I turned away from the plinth and walked toward the light of Frost's mage-globe, carrying the weight of what I'd seen and the growing certainty that this investigation would cost more than I could afford to pay.

But Grimsby had taught me that some debts were worth incurring.

And whoever had killed him—whoever was now harvesting bonds and building something terrible in the dark—they were about to learn that his student had inherited more than just his practise.

She'd inherited his stubbornness too.

Chapter 4: The Domestic Incursion

We emerged from the Warrens into grey afternoon light, blinking like creatures unaccustomed to the surface. The glamour sealed behind us, timber boards knitting back together as if we'd never passed through.

Frost checked his pocket watch—the gesture automatic, compulsive—then returned it to his waistcoat. "Analyst Green will process the workshop photographs tonight. I'll have preliminary findings by morning."

"And the symbol? The fist in chains?"

"I have sources who may recognise it." He didn't elaborate. "In the meantime, you should rest. Tomorrow we trace the secondary thread to its origin point."

"Where?"

"A warehouse district near Tower Bridge. The location registers as a thin place on our monitoring grid—Border Realm bleed. We'll need your Thread Sight to navigate safely."

I nodded, too exhausted to argue. The Warrens had drained something from me that sleep might not restore. Pip had gone silent on my shoulder, his small body heavy with the same weariness.

Halloway pulled the M.O.P. vehicle to the curb outside my Clerkenwell office. The kebab shop was doing brisk evening business, the smell of lamb and spices drifting up to where I stood on the pavement.

"Miss Blackwell." Frost had lowered his window. "I'll collect you at five tomorrow morning. The thread is most visible at dawn."

"I'll be ready."

The vehicle pulled away. I watched until it turned the corner, then climbed the narrow stairs to my office.

Clara was waiting.

She'd been stress-baking again—the flat smelled of chocolate and butter and the unmistakable sweetness of anxiety converted into confectionery. A seven-layer torte sat on the kitchen counter, elaborate enough to suggest she'd been at it for hours. She stood when I entered, wiping flour-dusted hands on her apron, eyes bright with questions she was trying not to ask.

"You're alive," she said.

"I'm alive."

"You look terrible."

"Thank you."

She crossed the room and pulled me into a hug before I could deflect. I stood rigid for a moment, then let myself lean into her warmth. Her cardigan smelled of vanilla extract and home.

"I made cake," she said into my shoulder. "And tea. And I reorganised the filing cabinet again because I didn't know what else to do."

"Pip will be devastated."

"Pip can file his complaints in triplicate." She released me and stepped back, studying my face with the careful attention she reserved for assessing damage. "What happened?"

I told her. Not everything—not Grimsby, not the workshop, not the symbol that still burned behind my eyes when I closed them—but enough. The Citadel. The case files. The Warrens and the people who lived there, forgotten by a system that preferred to pretend they didn't exist.

Clara listened without interrupting, her hands wrapped around a mug of tea she'd forgotten to drink. When I finished, she was quiet for a long moment.

"So you're working for them now," she said finally. "The M.O.P."

"With them. Not for them. There's a difference."

"Is there?"

I didn't have a good answer.

Clara stood and moved to the kitchen, cutting two slices of torte with more force than necessary. "I don't trust him. Frost. He's too... contained. Like a bomb that hasn't decided whether to go off yet."

"He's complicated."

"He's dangerous." She set a plate in front of me with a pointed clink. "And you're letting him into our life because he has leverage over you, which is exactly what men like him do. They find your weakness and they use it."

"Clara—"

"I've seen it before, Imogen. I married it." Her voice cracked slightly, then steadied. "Elias was charming too, at first. Polished. Said all the right things. And then the doors closed and the mask came off and—"

She stopped. Wrapped her arms around herself. The scars beneath her cardigan sleeves seemed to pulse with remembered pain.

I set down my fork and reached across the table. She let me take her hand.

"Frost isn't Elias."

"You don't know that."

"No," I admitted. "I don't. But I know that refusing to work with him means losing my certification, my practise, everything we've built here. And I know that someone is killing people using magic that shouldn't exist. And I know that Grimsby—" My voice caught. "Grimsby was investigating something before he died. Something connected to this. And Frost was ordered to bury it, and now he's trying to dig it back up."

Clara's hand tightened on mine. "You think he's on your side?"

"I think he's on his own side. But right now, his side and my side might be pointing in the same direction."

She was quiet for a moment. Then: "Eat your cake. You look like you haven't had a proper meal in days."

I ate. The chocolate was rich and dark, exactly what I needed. Clara watched me with the satisfaction of someone whose love language was feeding people.

Pip emerged from my document case, where he'd been sulking since the Warrens. He climbed onto the table and helped himself to a crumb of torte, his tiny face still pinched with displeasure.

"The Inspector is a complication," he announced. "I have updated his file accordingly."

"What file?"

"The file I keep on everyone who enters Miss Blackwell's life. Cross-referenced by threat level, usefulness, and probability of betrayal." He licked chocolate from his paw. "Inspector Frost currently registers as high on all three metrics."

"That's not reassuring."

"It is not meant to be reassuring. It is meant to be accurate." He fixed me with amber eyes. "The Warrens workshop disturbed you. I could feel it through your shoulder tension. What did you see that you didn't tell the Inspector?"

I hesitated. Clara leaned forward, sensing the weight of what I hadn't said.

"The symbol," I said slowly. "The fist wrapped in chains. I've seen it before."

"Where?"

"In Grimsby's notes. The ones he left me when he died." I pushed my plate away, appetite gone. "He was researching something called the Collector's Mark. A signature used by someone—or something—that specialized in harvesting magical debts. He never finished the research. He died before he could."

Clara's face had gone pale. "You think whoever killed Grimsby is connected to these murders?"

"I think Grimsby was getting close to something. Close enough that someone decided he needed to be silenced." I met her eyes. "And I think Frost knows more than he's telling me. He admitted he was ordered to close Grimsby's case. What he didn't say was why he's reopening it now—really reopening it. What changed?"

The question hung in the air between us.

A knock at the door made all three of us jump.

Clara rose, wiping her hands on her apron. She moved toward the door, then paused, looking back at me. I nodded, and she opened it.

Lord Nathaniel Frost stood in the doorway, still in his charcoal three-piece suit, still rigidly composed—but something about his posture suggested uncertainty. He held his hat in both hands at waist level, turning it slightly, the way he'd turned his pocket watch.

"Miss Vance." He inclined his head. "I apologise for the intrusion. Is Miss Blackwell available?"

Clara's expression flickered through several emotions: surprise, suspicion, and the particular wariness of someone assessing a potential threat—before settling on reluctant courtesy. "She's here. Come in, I suppose."

Frost entered the flat with the careful movements of someone navigating unfamiliar territory. His eyes swept the room, cataloguing details: the shabby furniture, the cluttered bookshelves, the filing cabinet with Pip's organizational system, the kitchen where Clara's baking supplies covered every surface.

He looked uncomfortable. It was the first time I'd seen him look anything other than perfectly controlled.

"Inspector." I stood but didn't approach. "Is there a development?"

"No. That is—" He stopped. Started again. "I came to deliver additional information regarding tomorrow's operation. The warehouse location is more unstable than initial reports suggested. I wanted to ensure you understood the risks before committing."

"You came to my home. At seven in the evening. To discuss operational risks."

A muscle twitched in his jaw. "I also wished to..." He trailed off, seemingly at a loss.

Clara, who had been watching this exchange with growing interest, stepped into the breach. "Inspector Frost. Would you like some tea? I've just made a fresh pot. And there's cake."

Frost blinked. The offer of tea appeared to have caught him entirely off guard.

"I—yes. Thank you, Miss Vance. That would be acceptable."

Clara guided him to the sofa with the same gentle insistence she used on nervous clients. She pressed a cup into his hands before he could refuse, then added a slice of torte on a plate balanced on the sofa arm.

"Thank you," he said again, holding the mismatched china with the careful precision of someone handling evidence. The delicate floral pattern looked absurd against his formal severity.

I remained standing, leaning against the kitchen doorframe, arms crossed. Watching.

Clara settled into her usual armchair, tucking her feet beneath her. "Imogen tells me you're investigating the blood oath murders. That must be dreadful work."

"It's necessary work."

"But dreadful nonetheless. Finding people after they've been killed like that."

"The M.O.P. employs specialists trained to manage the psychological impact of violent crime investigation."

I made a quiet observation about the effectiveness of M.O.P. psychological services, based on Sergeant Halloway's coffee consumption. Frost's mouth twitched—not quite a smile, but the closest I'd seen from him.

Clara asked about his education, his background, whether he preferred tea or coffee. She filled silences with questions, barely waiting for answers before launching into the next inquiry. It was her gift—making people talk despite themselves.

Frost answered each question with complete formal sentences that satisfied social requirements without revealing anything beneath them. But gradually, almost imperceptibly, his shoulders dropped. His grip on the teacup loosened. The rigid posture softened by degrees.

I was watching for it. I saw the moment something in him began to relax.

An hour passed. Maybe more. The light through the windows faded from grey to dark. Street lamps flickered on below.

Frost glanced at his pocket watch—checked it, closed it, then set it on the side table beside him instead of returning it to his pocket. The gesture was small, but I understood what it meant. He was choosing to stay rather than marking time until he could leave.

"The warehouse," he said finally, returning to what was ostensibly the purpose of his visit. "The Border Realm bleed creates instability. Reality becomes... negotiable in those spaces. If we encounter hostiles, standard defensive magic may not function as expected."

"I'm a Null," I reminded him. "Magic doesn't function as expected around me regardless."

"Which is precisely why I need you there. Your Thread Sight operates independently of the surrounding magical environment. You can see what my officers cannot." He paused, something flickering in his grey eyes. "But I wanted you to understand that I cannot guarantee your safety. The Border Realm is unpredictable. If circumstances require, I may have to prioritize the mission over protecting civilian assets."

"You're warning me that you might not be able to save me."

"I'm ensuring you enter this operation with accurate expectations."

Clara's hands had locked around her teacup, knuckles whitening.

I pushed off from the doorframe and crossed to sit in the chair opposite the sofa. Closer to Frost than I'd been all evening. Close enough to see the fine lines of tension around his eyes, the way his hands remained perfectly steady despite the conversation's weight.

"Why are you really here, Inspector?"

He met my gaze directly. The mask was still in place, but thinner now. Worn at the edges by an hour of Clara's relentless hospitality and the warmth of a flat that had nothing to do with power or politics.

"Because I sent you into danger today without adequate preparation. The Warrens were a calculated risk, but I did not fully brief you on what we might encounter. That was a failure of leadership." His jaw tightened. "I do not intend to repeat it."

"So this is an apology?"

"This is an acknowledgment of responsibility."

"That's a very formal way of saying sorry."

The corner of his mouth twitched again. "I am a very formal person."

Clara snorted quietly, then tried to disguise it as a cough.

Frost rose, setting his teacup down with precise care. He'd barely touched the cake, but he'd drunk three cups of tea—I'd counted. "I should go. Ward maintenance requires my attention this evening."

"The wards on Ashwood Manor?" I asked, remembering the way he checked his pocket watch compulsively, the way he'd mentioned his family's burden without explaining it.

Something shuttered in his expression. "Yes."

He collected his hat, performed a formal half-bow toward Clara. "Thank you for your hospitality, Miss Vance. The tea was excellent."

"Come back anytime," Clara said, and sounded like she meant it. "I always make too much."

At the door, Frost paused. Turned back. His eyes found mine across the room.

"Five o'clock," he said. "Don't be late."

Then he was gone.

Clara spun toward me immediately, eyes bright. "He stayed for over an hour. He checked his watch four times but kept finding reasons not to leave."

"He came to discuss the operation."

"He came to see you." She was nearly bouncing. "He barely touched the chocolate, Imogen. A man who turns down chocolate isn't thinking about cake."

I moved to clear the tea things, needing something to do with my hands. "The Inspector is a colleague. And a complicated one."

"Complicated how?"

I shut off the tap and turned to face her. "Because he represents everything I've spent five years fighting against. Because if he decides I'm more threat than asset, I lose everything. Because his sister died under circumstances he won't explain, and his family maintains something that requires him to check his watch like it's counting down to catastrophe."

Clara's expression softened. "You noticed all that."

"I notice everything. It's my job."

"It's not just your job." She leaned against the counter beside me. "He looks at you like you're a puzzle he can't solve. And you look at him like—"

"Don't."

"Like he might be worth solving too."

I dried my hands on the dishcloth, hung it precisely over the oven handle. "We have work to do tomorrow. Dangerous work. I need to sleep."

Clara recognised the deflection. She let me have it.

"Be careful," she said quietly. "With the warehouse. With all of it."

"I will."

I retreated to my room, but sleep was a long time coming. I lay in the dark, listening to Clara move through the flat, to Pip's small sounds as he settled into his filing cabinet nest, to the city breathing beyond the window.

Frost's face kept surfacing in my mind. The way his mask had slipped, just slightly, in the warmth of our shabby flat. The way he'd set down his pocket watch instead of keeping it close. The way he'd said I *cannot guarantee your safety* like the admission cost him something.

He was dangerous. Clara was right about that.

But he was also the first person in five years who'd looked at my work—my illegal, impossible, necessary work—and seen something worth protecting rather than something worth prosecuting.

I didn't know what to do with that.

So I did what I always did with things I didn't understand: I filed them away for later analysis and forced myself to sleep.

Tomorrow would bring the warehouse. The Border Realm. Whatever waited in the spaces where reality grew thin.

I would need all my strength to face it.

Chapter 5: The Ambush at the Threshold

The M.O.P. vehicle pulled to the curb outside my office at half past four, fifteen minutes early. I'd been watching from the window for twenty, unable to sleep past three.

Frost emerged from the passenger side as I descended the stairs. In the pre-dawn darkness, his charcoal suit looked black, his face carved from shadow and streetlight. He opened my door without comment.

I slid into the back seat. Duan sat beside me, her forensic kit between her feet, dark circles carved beneath her eyes. Halloway drove, his bulk filling the driver's seat, hands steady on the wheel.

No one spoke as we crossed London.

The city was different at this hour—empty streets, shuttered shops, the heavy silence of a world holding its breath before waking. We passed through the City's glass towers, crossed the Thames at Tower Bridge, turned into the warehouse district that spread along the river's southern bank like a scar.

Frost checked his pocket watch twice during the drive. The gesture had become familiar—open, glance, close, return. A ritual that meant something I didn't yet understand.

"The thread," he said finally, breaking the silence. "Is it still visible?"

I removed my spectacles and activated Thread Sight. The world stripped to its architecture—golden filaments crisscrossing the streets, red oaths glowing from government buildings in the distance, the silver-blue of civic duty threads stretching toward Westminster.

And there, faint but persistent, the golden marriage thread I'd traced from the Warrens. It extended eastward, pulsing weakly, leading toward a derelict structure three blocks ahead.

"Still visible. But fading. We have maybe an hour before it degrades completely."

"Then we move quickly."

Halloway parked on a concrete apron outside a warehouse that looked like it had been dying for decades. Three stories of blackened brick, windows shattered or boarded, roof partially collapsed. A loading dock gaped open, exhaling cold air that had nothing to do with the October morning.

We disembarked into silence.

The temperature dropped the moment my feet touched the ground—not natural chill but something deeper, wronger. The kind of cold that suggested we'd crossed an invisible boundary into territory where normal rules had been quietly suspended.

"Border Realm bleed," Duan said quietly, consulting a device I didn't recognise. "Stronger than the reports indicated. Reality's thin here."

Halloway checked his warding stones, testing each against his palm. They flared briefly, confirming active magic. Frost stood motionless, surveying the warehouse with the focused attention of a predator assessing terrain.

"The thread leads inside," I said. "Through the loading dock."

Frost nodded once. "Standard formation. I take point. Halloway, rear guard. Duan, document what you can. Miss Blackwell—"

"Stay close and don't engage hostiles. I remember."

His eyes met mine in the grey light. Something flickered there—acknowledgment, perhaps, or warning. "This location is unstable. If I give an order, follow it without question. There won't be time for debate."

"Understood."

He moved toward the loading dock, and we followed.

The interior was worse than the exterior suggested. Collapsed beams created obstacle courses of debris. Rusted machinery loomed in the darkness like the skeletons of industrial giants. The air tasted of mold and old magic and something metallic I couldn't identify.

The golden thread led deeper, pulsing faintly, guiding us through the maze.

"There." Frost's voice was barely above a whisper. He pointed toward a doorway at the far end of the main floor—a threshold that shimmered with ward-work, reality bending visibly around its edges.

I examined it with Thread Sight. The ward appeared as a vertical seam of compressed golden threads, woven so tightly they created an actual barrier. Ancient work, skilled, the magical equivalent of a contract clause written in dead languages.

"Someone's been using this place," I said. "The ward's been maintained recently. Within the last week."

"Can you breach it?"

"I'm a Null. Wards don't stop me—they just make themselves known." I stepped toward the threshold. "But whoever's inside will know we've arrived the moment I cross."

Frost considered this. Then: "Duan, Halloway. Defensive positions. Miss Blackwell, you cross first. I follow immediately. Whatever's on the other side, we handle it together."

I approached the threshold. The ward pressed against my chest, my face, like pushing through heavy curtains soaked in something cold and faintly repulsive. My ears popped. Resistance without substance, wrongness without pain.

Then release.

The space beyond was impossible.

The warehouse interior had expanded into something that shouldn't exist—a cavernous hall stretching hundreds of feet in every direction, the ceiling lost in grey fog, the walls flickering between brick and stone and something organic that pulsed faintly with its own light. The Border Realm bleed had created a pocket dimension, reality folded back on itself like a contract with hidden clauses.

The golden thread terminated at a stone altar in the center of the space.

And standing beside the altar, waiting, was a man I'd never seen before.

Tall, gaunt, wearing robes that seemed to absorb light rather than reflect it. His face was angular, predatory, with eyes that gleamed red in the grey fog. He smiled when he saw me—a smile that held no warmth, only anticipation.

"The Scribe." His voice echoed strangely, coming from multiple directions at once. "I wondered when Frost would find someone capable of following the threads. You're earlier than I expected."

Frost materialized beside me, ice already forming on his fingertips. "Julian Vane. You're under arrest for the murders of Marcus Bellingham, Edmund Cartwright, and Elias Thorne."

Vane. The name triggered something in my memory—one of Grimsby's notes, a reference to a family with connections to pre-Reformation artifacts. But I couldn't place it, not with my heart hammering and magic crackling in the air around us.

Julian Vane laughed. "Arrest. How quaint. You bring four people into my domain and you think you're making an arrest?"

"Five," said Halloway, stepping through the threshold behind us. Duan followed, her silver binding chains already in hand.

Vane's smile didn't waver. "Four, five—it doesn't matter. You're in the Border Realm now, Inspector. Your jurisdiction ended at the threshold."

He raised his hand.

The world fractured.

I dropped to the ground as something screamed past my head—not a physical projectile but a tear in reality itself, a wound in the air that bled grey light. Frost's ice erupted in a defensive wall, crystalline and sharp, deflecting a second attack that would have taken Duan in the chest.

Halloway charged forward with a roar, his warding stones blazing. Vane gestured lazily, and the sergeant flew backward, slamming into a pillar that shouldn't have been there a moment ago. He crumpled, blood streaming from a gash at his temple.

"Halloway!" Duan's voice cracked with fear, but she held her position, chains whirling in defensive patterns.

Frost pressed the attack, ice magic surging from his hands in controlled bursts. The temperature plummeted. His breath clouded white. Frost crept up his sleeves, his collar, creeping toward his face with each expenditure of power.

Vane deflected each strike with contemptuous ease, reality bending around him like a shield. He was drawing power from the Border Realm itself, I realised—feeding on the instability, using it as an endless reserve.

"You can't win this, Frost." Vane's voice carried over the chaos. "You're fighting on my ground, with my rules. Did you really think institutional authority would matter here?"

I scrambled behind a pillar, mind racing. Vane was too powerful, too well-prepared. We'd walked into a trap, and now we were dying in it.

Thread Sight showed me what mundane vision couldn't. The golden threads of Vane's power, thick as cables, anchoring him to the Border Realm's instability. The red threads of blood oaths binding the space to his will. And there—faint but present—a single thread connecting him to something beyond the altar.

A contract. He was bound to this place through a contract.

I reached for the thread without thinking. My hand passed through empty air—Nulls could see threads, but we couldn't touch them. Couldn't manipulate them.

Except.

Grimsby's training surfaced through the panic. *Nulls can't affect threads directly. But with physical contact, with concentration, we can sometimes fray what others have bound. It's dangerous. It's forbidden. And it might save your life someday.*

I hadn't done it in years. Hadn't needed to. But Halloway was down, Duan was barely holding, and Frost was burning through his reserves faster than he could sustain.

I ran.

Vane saw me coming—his eyes widened with surprise, then amusement. "The Scribe wants to play? How delightful."

He raised his hand toward me. Reality twisted.

Frost's ice wall erupted between us, taking the attack meant for my chest. The impact shattered the barrier and sent him staggering, frost burns spreading across his palms where he'd channeled too much power too quickly.

But it gave me the second I needed.

I grabbed Vane's wrist.

The contact was electric—magic surging against my Null status, trying to reject me, finding no purchase. I could feel his binding thread now, the contract that anchored him to this place. It pulsed against my palm like a living thing.

Grimsby would have called what I was about to do unauthorised practise of advocacy—making a legal argument with my hands instead of my voice, enforcing a contract's termination clause without standing to do so. The Ethics Committee would have called it something worse.

I frayed it anyway.

Not breaking—I couldn't break a thread this strong—but weakening, compromising, introducing instability into the perfect architecture of his binding. The threads thinned and crossed at wrong angles, exactly like the debt clauses I sabotaged in my office, exactly like the work Grimsby had taught me.

Vane screamed.

His power flickered. The reality-bending attacks stuttered and failed. For one moment, he was just a man—shocked, vulnerable, the foundation of his strength crumbling beneath him.

Frost's ice took him in the chest.

The impact threw Vane backward into the altar. He hit stone with a crack that might have been bone, slid to the ground, and didn't rise.

For a moment, everything was still.

Then the Border Realm began to collapse.

"Out!" Frost's voice cut through the ringing in my ears. "The threshold's destabilizing! Move!"

Duan grabbed Halloway, hauling his semiconscious weight across her shoulders with strength that belied her slight frame. I ran for the doorway, the ground shifting beneath my feet, walls flickering between states of reality.

The threshold was shrinking. The ward-work that had held this space together was failing, the seams of compressed threads unraveling as Vane's binding collapsed.

Duan dove through first, Halloway in tow. I was three steps behind—two—one—

The world lurched.

I felt myself falling, the threshold closing around me like a fist, reality squeezing tight—

Arms caught me. Cold arms, strong arms, pulling me through the impossible space between moments. Ice crackled against my skin. Someone's body covered mine as the threshold collapsed completely, sealing the pocket dimension away forever.

We hit concrete. Hard.

I lay on the warehouse floor, gasping, my ribs screaming where I'd impacted the ground. Above me, the doorway that had led to the Border Realm was simply... gone. Brick wall, unbroken, as if the threshold had never existed.

Frost lay beside me, his arms still wrapped around my torso.

His hands were shaking. Fine tremors running through his fingers, his wrists, visible even in the dim light of the pre-dawn warehouse. Frost burns covered his palms—raw red wounds where ice magic had eaten through gloves and skin.

He'd pulled me through the collapsing threshold. He'd shielded me with his body when the dimensional pocket sealed.

He'd chosen my survival over his own safety.

"Inspector." My voice came out rough. "Your hands."

"Acceptable damage." He released me and sat up slowly, examining his burned palms with clinical detachment. "Duan. Halloway's status."

"Concussion, probably." Duan's voice came from somewhere to my left. "Needs medical attention. The sergeant's awake but not coherent."

"Vehicle. Now. We need extraction before anyone comes to investigate the magical signature."

We moved. Halloway between Duan and Frost, stumbling but mobile. I brought up the rear, my legs unsteady, my mind still processing what had happened.

What I had done.

I'd frayed Julian Vane's binding thread. I'd used forbidden Null techniques in front of M.O.P. officers. Frost had watched me do it—had watched my hand close around Vane's wrist, had seen the moment when impossible magic became possible through my touch.

He knew now. He knew what I could do.

And he'd saved my life anyway.

We reached the vehicle. Duan loaded Halloway into the back seat, climbing in beside him to monitor his condition. Frost took the driver's seat, his burned hands gripping the wheel with visible pain.

I slid into the passenger seat and stared straight ahead.

No one spoke as we drove away from the warehouse.

The sky was lightening to grey in the east. London was waking around us—commuters beginning their journeys, shops preparing to open, the mundane world continuing its routine entirely unaware that a pocket dimension had just collapsed three miles away.

Frost checked his pocket watch. The gesture was automatic, but I saw the way his hand trembled, the way the silver case rattled against his frost-damaged palm.

"Miss Blackwell." His voice was controlled, but something underneath it wasn't. "What you did to Vane's binding."

"I know."

"That technique is forbidden. The High Council considers it grounds for immediate certification revocation."

"I know."

Silence. The vehicle hummed through empty streets.

"I will not be including it in my report."

I turned to look at him. His profile was rigid, jaw tight, eyes fixed on the road ahead. The frost burns on his hands were already blistering.

"Why?"

He was quiet for a long moment. Then: "Because you saved Duan's life. And Halloway's. And quite possibly mine." A pause. "Because the technique worked, and sometimes what works matters more than what's permitted."

"That doesn't sound like institutional thinking."

"No." His mouth twitched—that almost-smile I was learning to recognise. "It doesn't."

We drove the rest of the way in silence, but something had shifted between us. Some wall had developed a crack.

I didn't know yet whether that was dangerous or simply unprecedented.

Probably both.

The M.O.P. safehouse was a nondescript building in Whitechapel, warded to the ceiling and staffed by officers who asked no questions. Duan took Halloway to the medical bay while Frost led me to a small kitchen that smelled of stale coffee and industrial cleaning solution.

He sat at the metal table and began unwrapping his burned hands, movements precise despite the tremors. I found a first aid kit in a cabinet and set it beside him without asking permission.

"I can manage."

"Your hands are shaking too badly to apply bandages." I pulled out burn cream and gauze. "Let me."

He hesitated—I could see the resistance, the reluctance to accept help—then extended his right hand toward me.

The frost burns were worse than I'd realised. Raw, weeping wounds that would scar without proper treatment. I applied the cream carefully, trying not to cause more pain, acutely aware of how close we sat. His fingers were long, elegant despite the damage. Cold radiated from his skin even now, residual magic bleeding off in waves.

"In the warehouse," I said quietly, focusing on the bandaging. "When the threshold collapsed. You could have shielded yourself. Your ice responds faster when you're not dividing your attention."

"Yes."

"You chose to shield me instead."

His hand tensed under my fingers, then deliberately relaxed. "Yes."

"Why?"

Frost was silent for a long moment. I finished wrapping his right hand and moved to his left, repeating the process. Cream, gauze, careful pressure.

"I don't know," he said finally. His voice was rough. "It wasn't tactical. It wasn't procedure. Procedure would have been to protect myself and trust that a Null could survive threshold collapse without assistance."

"But you didn't."

"No."

I tied off the last bandage and looked up. His grey eyes met mine, and in them I saw something I hadn't expected—uncertainty. Vulnerability. The controlled mask cracked just enough to show what lay beneath.

"I find myself making choices around you that I cannot explain through institutional logic," he said quietly. "I'm not certain whether that's dangerous or simply unprecedented."

My chest tightened. The smart response was to deflect—remind him that we were colleagues, that personal entanglement complicated professional obligation, that I didn't trust the M.O.P. and shouldn't trust him.

Instead I said, "Both, probably."

His mouth quirked. That almost-smile, closer to the surface now. "Yes. Probably both."

The moment stretched. Neither of us moved. The fluorescent lights hummed overhead. Somewhere in the building, a door slammed.

Then footsteps in the corridor—Duan returning with a status update on Halloway—and Frost stepped back. The mask slid into place, controlled and professional.

But something had shifted. Some wall had developed a crack.

I returned my attention to the first aid kit, packing supplies away with careful precision, and pretended my hands weren't shaking too.

Miller arrived an hour later, rumpled and irritable and carrying a folder of financial records he'd spent the night compiling. He spread papers across the safehouse table while Duan made coffee strong enough to dissolve spoons.

"Julian Vane," Miller said, tapping a photograph. "Born 1985, minor branch of the Vane family. No significant magical ability recorded, which makes him an odd choice for reality-bending combat."

"He was drawing power from the Border Realm," I said. "Using the instability as a reserve. That's not natural ability—that's artifact-assisted."

"Which matches what we found at the Warrens workshop." Frost stood at the window, his bandaged hands clasped behind his back. "Someone has been collecting power from severed marriage bonds. Vane was using that power to fuel his operations."

"But Vane's not the mastermind," Miller continued. "Financial records show payments coming into his accounts from an external source. Regular deposits, significant amounts, starting approximately eighteen months ago."

"When the first modifications appeared in the marriage contracts," I said. "Someone's been funding this operation from the beginning."

Duan pulled up images on her tablet. "The symbol from the Warrens workshop—the fist wrapped in chains. I found references in pre-Reformation texts. It's called the Collector's Mark. Used by practitioners who specialized in harvesting magical debts."

"Harvesting," Frost repeated. "Not just collecting. Converting debt into usable power."

"Which explains why they're targeting wealthy marriages," I said. The pieces were clicking together now, forming a picture I didn't want to see. "Soul-linked bonds between ancient bloodlines contain enormous magical investment. Severing them releases that power. Someone's been systematically extracting it."

"For what purpose?"

I thought of the symbol. The converging threads. The careful, patient architecture of something being built in darkness.

"I don't know yet. But whatever they're building, they need a lot of power to do it. More than three marriages can provide."

Miller flipped to another page in his folder. "Vane's accounts show forty-three additional families flagged for 'consultation services.' All newly married. All with significant magical lineages."

Forty-three families. Forty-three potential targets.

"We need to warn them," Duan said.

"We need to find whoever's funding Vane first." Frost turned from the window. "He's a tool, not the architect. If we alert the targets before identifying the mastermind, they'll simply find another method."

"And in the meantime, people keep dying."

"In the meantime, we work faster." His grey eyes found mine across the room. "Miss Blackwell. You said you'd seen the Collector's Mark before. In Grimsby's notes."

"Yes."

"I need access to those notes."

I hesitated. Grimsby's research was private—the only thing I had left of my mentor, carefully preserved in my locked drawer for five years. Sharing it with M.O.P. felt like betrayal.

But Grimsby had died trying to expose systematic exploitation. And now that same system was being harvested by someone willing to kill for power.

"Tonight," I said. "Come to my office after dark. I'll show you everything."

Frost nodded once. Something passed between us—acknowledgment, perhaps, or the beginning of trust.

"Then we have work to do." He collected his coat, movements careful around his bandaged hands. "Duan, continue processing the warehouse evidence. Miller, trace Vane's funding source. Miss Blackwell, rest while you can. Tonight, we dig into the past."

He left without looking back, but I felt his attention linger.

I sat at the table surrounded by evidence of conspiracy and murder, forty-three families marked for death, and the growing certainty that Grimsby's unfinished work was now mine to complete.

Whatever he'd discovered, whatever had got him killed—I was going to find it.

And whoever was behind this, whoever had been building something terrible in the darkness for eighteen months—they were going to learn that Marcus Grimsby had trained his student well.

Some debts couldn't be escaped.

Some bonds couldn't be severed.

And some wrongs demanded accounting, no matter how powerful the people responsible believed themselves to be.

I gathered my things and prepared to go home. Clara would be worried. Pip would have filed seventeen complaints about my absence.

And tonight, Nathaniel Frost would walk into my office, and I would show him the research that had killed my mentor.

The investigation was just beginning.

Chapter 6: The Mentor's Research

Clara had stress-baked three dozen scones by the time I got home.

The flat smelled of butter and rosemary and barely-controlled panic. She stood at the kitchen counter, flour dusting her cardigan sleeves, hands working dough with a violence of someone converting fear into pastry.

"You're alive," she said without turning around.

"I'm alive."

"You were supposed to be back hours ago."

"The operation ran long."

She spun to face me, and I saw the tear tracks on her cheeks, the redness around her eyes. "The operation ran long. That's what you're giving me? I've been here since dawn imagining every terrible thing that could have happened, and you walk in and say the operation ran long?"

"Clara—"

"No." She held up a flour-covered hand. "No, you don't get to 'Clara' me. You left before sunrise to chase murderers into some magical death trap, and then you disappeared for eight hours without a single message, and I had to sit here and wait and wonder if you were dead in a ditch somewhere because you're too stubborn to ask for help and too proud to admit when you're in over your head—"

Her voice cracked. She pressed her hands against the counter, shoulders shaking.

I crossed the kitchen and pulled her into my arms.

She resisted for a moment—pride, anger, the same stubbornness she was accusing me of—then crumpled against my chest. Her tears soaked through my blouse. I held her and said nothing, because there was nothing to say. She was right. I'd been thoughtless, and she'd been terrified, and no amount of explanation would undo those hours of fear.

"I'm sorry," I said finally. "I should have sent word."

"Yes. You should have."

"I'll do better."

She pulled back, wiping her eyes with her flour-dusted sleeve, leaving white streaks across her cheeks. "You'd better. I can't lose you too, Imogen. I can't."

The weight of what she wasn't saying hung between us. Her marriage. Her escape. The years of abuse she'd survived before finding her way to my office door with nothing but a battered suitcase and a desperate need for help.

I'd saved her then. She'd saved me in return, in ways I'd never admitted aloud.

"You won't lose me," I said. "I promise."

"Don't make promises you can't keep."

"I keep all my promises. Ask any of my clients."

She laughed—a wet, broken sound that was better than tears. "You're impossible."

"I've been told."

Pip emerged from the filing cabinet where he'd been hiding during Clara's outburst. He climbed onto the counter and surveyed the scone production with professional interest.

"Miss Vance has produced enough baked goods to feed a small army," he observed. "I have catalogued each batch by flavor profile and structural integrity. The rosemary specimens are superior to the cheddar, though both exceed acceptable parameters for consumption."

"Thank you, Pip," Clara said, her voice still thick. "That's... very thorough."

"Thoroughness is my purpose." He fixed me with amber eyes. "Miss Blackwell. You are injured."

I looked down at myself. Scrapes on my palms from the warehouse floor. A bruise forming on my shoulder where I'd hit concrete. The general dishevelment of someone who'd nearly been killed by a reality-bending madman.

"Minor damage," I said. "Nothing serious."

"I will update your medical file accordingly." He hopped down and disappeared into his filing cabinet, muttering about inadequate self-preservation instincts.

Clara turned back to her scones, shaping the dough with more controlled movements now. "What happened? Can you tell me?"

I leaned against the counter beside her, watching her work. "We found the man responsible for the murders. There was a confrontation. He's in custody now."

"And the investigation is over?"

"No." I thought of Julian Vane, of the funding source Miller couldn't trace, of the forty-three families still at risk. "He was working for someone. The investigation continues."

Clara nodded slowly. Her hands had steadied, the rhythm of baking providing the comfort it always did. "The Inspector. Frost. He kept you safe?"

"He—" I stopped, remembering ice walls and burned palms and arms wrapped around me as reality collapsed. "Yes. He did."

She glanced at me, something knowing in her expression. "You like him."

"I don't—"

"Imogen." She set down the dough and turned to face me fully. "I've known you for two years. I've seen you interact with hundreds of clients, dozens of officials, countless people who wanted something from you. You don't look at any of them the way you look at him."

"How do I look at him?"

"Like he might be worth trusting." She reached out and squeezed my hand, leaving flour prints on my fingers. "That scares you."

I didn't have a response to that.

"He's coming here tonight," I said instead. "Inspector Frost. I agreed to show him Grimsby's research notes. The ones from before his death."

Clara's eyes widened. "You're showing him Marcus's files? The private ones?"

"The investigation requires it. Grimsby was researching the same patterns we're seeing now—systematic exploitation, debt harvesting, bond manipulation. His work might contain information that identifies whoever is behind this."

"And you trust Frost enough to share that with him?"

I thought about it. Really thought, past the institutional wariness and professional caution and the instinct that had kept me safe for five years.

"I think I'm starting to," I admitted.

Clara studied my face for a long moment. Then she nodded, as if I'd confirmed something she'd already suspected.

"I'll make dinner," she said. "Something hearty. He looks like a man who doesn't eat properly."

"Clara, you don't have to—"

"I'm making dinner." Her voice brooked no argument. "If you're going to invite a dangerous M.O.P. Inspector into our home to review your dead mentor's secret research, the least I can do is ensure everyone is fed."

I didn't argue. There was no point arguing with Clara when she'd decided to feed someone.

Frost arrived at seven, precisely on time.

He'd changed from his charcoal suit into something darker—black wool, more severe, though still impeccably tailored. His hands were wrapped in fresh bandages, and he moved them carefully as Clara took his coat.

"Inspector," she said. "Welcome. I've made lamb stew."

Frost blinked, clearly not having expected dinner. "That's very kind, Miss Vance. Thank you."

"It's no trouble. Imogen tells me you've been keeping her alive, which earns you at least one hot meal."

She led him to the small dining table, where she'd set three places with our mismatched china. The stew steamed in a ceramic pot at the center, surrounded by fresh bread and butter and a bottle of wine I didn't remember buying.

Frost sat where directed, looking almost comically out of place in our shabby flat—all sharp angles and aristocratic composure against the faded floral wallpaper and second-hand furniture. But he picked up his spoon when Clara served him and ate without complaint, even complimenting the seasoning with what appeared to be genuine appreciation.

I watched them interact over the meal, Clara filling silences with gentle questions, Frost responding with his careful formality that gradually softened as the wine flowed and the food warmed. It was strange, seeing him here. In the Citadel, in the warehouse, even in the safehouse kitchen, he'd seemed like a force of nature—powerful, remote, untouchable.

Here, eating lamb stew from a chipped bowl while Clara told him about her bread-baking experiments, he seemed almost human.

Pip observed from his filing cabinet perch, making notes in a tiny ledger he'd produced from somewhere. I didn't want to know what categories he was tracking.

After dinner, Clara cleared the dishes with pointed efficiency. "I'll be in my room with a book. Call if you need anything."

She kissed my cheek as she passed—a gesture of support and warning combined—and disappeared down the hallway.

Frost and I were alone.

"Your flatmate is formidable," he said.

"She's protective." I stood and moved toward my locked desk drawer. "She's also right—I don't eat properly when she's not here to enforce it."

"Neither do I." The admission seemed to surprise him as much as it surprised me.

I produced the key from its hiding place and unlocked the drawer. Inside, beneath the Null-Ink supplies and client files that could never see daylight, lay a leather folder worn soft with age.

Marcus Grimsby's research.

I lifted it carefully and carried it to the desk, setting it down between us. The leather was cracked at the corners, the pages inside yellow with time. Five years of grief pressed against my chest.

"He gave this to me the week before he died," I said quietly. "Told me to keep it safe, to study it, to continue his work if anything happened to him. I thought he was being dramatic. He was always a bit theatrical about the importance of what we did."

"And then he died."

"And then he was murdered." I opened the folder. "I read through it after his funeral. I understood maybe half of what he'd documented. The rest seemed like paranoid conspiracy—patterns he thought he saw, connections he couldn't prove. I filed it away and focused on surviving."

"Until now."

"Until now."

Frost moved to stand beside me, close enough that I could feel the cold radiating from his skin. Whatever magic he carried, it lived in him always, ice lurking just beneath the surface.

We looked down at Grimsby's notes together.

The first pages were lists. Names, dates, contract references—dozens of them, organised in Grimsby's precise handwriting. I recognised some: families I'd helped, cases he'd mentioned during my training, names that appeared in Scribe Guild records.

"These are all working-class supernatural beings," I said, tracing the entries. "Werewolves, minor fae, hedge witches. People without powerful family connections."

"Victims?"

"Clients." I turned pages. "Grimsby was documenting a pattern. Look—each entry includes a contract reference, a date, and a notation about 'structural irregularities.' He was tracking predatory lending. Debt servitude schemes. The same exploitative practises I've been fighting for five years."

Frost leaned closer, his shoulder nearly touching mine. "But this goes beyond individual cases."

"Yes." I found the section I remembered, the part that had seemed like conspiracy theory when I'd first read it. "He thought it was organised. Systematic. Multiple Council families using identical contract architecture to extract labor and power from working-class citizens."

The pages showed diagrams now—thread patterns, binding structures, the visual language of magical obligation rendered in ink and speculation. Grimsby had mapped the flow of power from debtor to creditor, tracing it upward through layers of shell companies and family trusts.

At the top of his diagram, a single symbol: a fist wrapped in chains.

The Collector's Mark.

"He knew," Frost said quietly. "Five years ago, Grimsby identified the same system we're seeing now."

"He was going to present evidence to the High Council. Proof that powerful families were coordinating exploitation rather than just coincidentally using similar methods." I stared at the symbol, remembering the Warrens workshop, the converging threads. "He died the night before his testimony was scheduled."

"And someone ordered the investigation closed."

"Yes." I looked up at him. "You said you were the investigating officer. You said you were told to stop. Who gave that order?"

Frost's jaw tightened. For a moment, I thought he wouldn't answer.

"Lady Augusta Stern," he said finally. "Chairwoman of the High Council's Oversight Committee. My aunt."

The words landed like stones dropped into still water. Ripples spreading outward, disturbing everything.

"Your aunt."

"She raised me after my parents died. She sits on the Council that governs supernatural London. She gave me a direct order to close the investigation and accept the official finding of accidental ward failure." His voice was flat, controlled. "I obeyed."

"And now?"

"Now I have three more bodies and evidence that the system she ordered me to protect is harvesting people for power." He turned away from the desk, moving toward the window. "The Vane family has connections to Lady Augusta's faction. Julian was likely recruited through those channels. If the funding source leads where I think it leads—"

"You'll be investigating your own family."

"Yes."

I watched his reflection in the dark glass—the rigid set of his shoulders, the careful stillness of a man holding himself together through will alone.

"That's why you brought me in," I said slowly. "Not just because my name was in Thorne's papers. Because you needed someone outside the system. Someone who couldn't be controlled through institutional pressure. Someone who would keep investigating even if the evidence pointed at the Council itself."

He turned to face me. In the lamplight, his grey eyes looked almost silver.

"You're the only Scribe in London who's spent five years proving you can't be bought or intimidated," he said. "The only one who helps the people the system is designed to crush. The only one Marcus Grimsby trained to see what others miss." A pause. "You're the only one I could trust with this."

The admission hung between us—raw, unexpected, more vulnerable than anything he'd shown me before.

"You trust me," I said.

"I'm beginning to."

"Even knowing what I can do. The thread-fraying. The forbidden techniques."

"Perhaps especially because of that." He crossed toward me, stopping at the edge of the desk. Close enough to touch, if either of us dared. "You break rules when breaking them serves justice. You protect people who have no other protection. You continue fighting even when the system is designed for you to fail." His voice dropped. "I spent twenty years believing the system could be reformed from within. You've spent five years proving that some things can only be changed by those willing to work outside it."

"That sounds like heresy, Inspector. The M.O.P. might revoke your credentials."

His mouth quirked—that almost-smile, closer now than I'd ever seen it. "Then I suppose I'll have to trust you to keep my secrets as well."

The moment stretched. The flat was quiet around us—Clara's door closed, Pip silent in his cabinet, the city breathing beyond the window. In this small space, surrounded by Grimsby's research and the weight of everything we'd discovered, something shifted.

He raised his hand, slowly, giving me time to pull away. His bandaged fingers hovered near my cheek—the same gesture he'd made in the safe-house, the same restraint.

This time, I leaned into his palm.

His breath caught. His hand curved against my face, cool despite the bandages, and his eyes searched mine with an intensity that made my chest tight.

"Imogen." My name in his voice sounded like a contract. Like a binding. Like something neither of us had agreed to but couldn't seem to refuse.

"Nathaniel."

His thumb brushed my cheekbone. The touch sent sparks across my skin, heat blooming where his coolness met my warmth.

I rose onto my toes—

A crash from Clara's room shattered the moment.

We broke apart, instinct overriding everything else. Frost's hand went to his waistcoat pocket; I grabbed the letter opener from my desk, the closest thing to a weapon I had.

"Clara?" I called.

No response.

I moved toward the hallway, Frost close behind. Clara's door stood closed, light visible beneath it, but no sound came from within.

I pushed it open.

Clara stood in the center of her room, pale as chalk, a photograph clutched in her trembling hands. At her feet, a shattered picture frame—the crash we'd heard. Her eyes were fixed on something I couldn't see, her expression one of absolute horror.

"Clara." I crossed to her, gripping her shoulders. "What happened? What's wrong?"

She raised the photograph, turning it so I could see.

My blood froze.

The image showed a group of people at a formal event—black tie, champagne glasses, the kind of aristocratic gathering that populated Society pages. And in the center of the group, his arm around a young woman I barely recognised...

Elias Thorne. The first victim. Smiling at the camera.

And the woman beside him—younger, thinner, with fear hiding behind her social smile—was Clara.

"I didn't know," she whispered. "I didn't know his family name. He just called himself Eli when we were together. Eli Stone. I didn't know he was a Thorne until I saw the papers today, the news about the investigation, and I found this old photo and—"

Her voice broke. She crumpled, and I caught her before she hit the floor.

Over her shaking shoulders, I met Frost's eyes. His expression had gone cold, professional—but beneath it, I saw the wheels turning. The implications assembling.

Clara had been married to Elias Thorne.

Clara lived with me.

Clara's name was nowhere in the official records—she'd fled, changed her identity, hidden from the husband who'd made her life a nightmare.

And now that husband was dead, murdered by the same conspiracy we were investigating, and Clara was connected to it all.

"Miss Vance." Frost's voice was carefully neutral. "I think you need to tell us everything."

Clara looked up at him through tears, her face a mask of old terror resurfacing.

"I can't," she whispered. "If anyone finds out I was married to him—if they know I escaped—"

"They won't." I tightened my arms around her. "Nathaniel, she's not a suspect. She's a survivor."

"I understand that." His grey eyes held mine. "But if she was married to Elias Thorne, she may have information about his contracts, his associates, his enemies. Information that could identify who's behind these murders."

Clara shuddered against me. "I don't know anything. I ran. Three years ago, I ran and I never looked back."

"Then tell us what you do know." I pulled back, cupping her face in my hands. "Clara. Look at me. Whatever happened between you and Elias—whatever he did to you—we're going to stop the people responsible for all of this. But we need to understand the connections. We need to know what he was involved in."

She swallowed hard. Nodded.

"Okay," she said shakily. "Okay. I'll tell you."

Frost produced his leather notebook. I guided Clara to sit on the edge of her bed.

And in the quiet of her small room, surrounded by the evidence of her new life, Clara began to tell us about her old one.

The marriage that had almost destroyed her.

The husband who was now a murder victim.

And the system of exploitation that had bound them together—the same system that had killed my mentor, that was killing wealthy purebloods now, that was building toward something terrible in the darkness.

The investigation had just become personal.

And nothing would be the same again.

Chapter 7: The Marriage That Was

Clara's hands shook as she cradled the tea I'd pressed into them. She sat on the edge of her bed, diminished somehow, the confident woman who'd lectured me about self-care reduced to someone I barely recognised.

Frost had pulled the vanity chair to face her, his notebook open on his knee. He'd removed his jacket, rolled his sleeves to reveal the bandages on his forearms—small concessions to informality that I suspected were deliberate. Making himself less intimidating. Less official.

I sat beside Clara on the bed, close enough that our shoulders touched. Grounding her. Reminding her she wasn't alone.

"Take your time," I said quietly. "Start wherever feels right."

Clara stared into her tea. The steam rose in delicate curls, catching the lamplight.

"I met him at a charity gala," she said finally. "Four years ago. I was working as an event coordinator—mundane work, nothing magical. I didn't even know supernatural society existed until Eli walked up to me with a glass of champagne and a smile that made me forget every warning my mother ever gave me about charming men."

"Eli Stone," Frost said. "Not Elias Thorne."

"He introduced himself as Eli Stone. Said he was in property development. Which was technically true, I suppose—the Thorne family owns half of Mayfair." Her laugh was bitter. "He told me later that he used the alias when he wanted to meet people who didn't know his family name. Said he wanted someone who liked him for himself, not his money."

"When did you learn his real identity?"

"After the wedding." Clara's grip tightened on the cup. "We eloped. He said it was romantic—just the two of us, no family pressure, no society obligations. I thought he was being spontaneous. I didn't realise he was hiding me."

I reached over and covered her hand with mine. She let me.

"The ceremony was magical," she continued. "Literally magical. A registrar I'd never seen before, words I didn't understand, a contract I signed without reading because Eli said it was just legal formalities." Her voice cracked. "I didn't know what I was signing. I didn't know contracts could bind more than property."

"A soul-linked marriage bond," I said. "Without your informed consent."

"I didn't even know such things existed. I was mundane, Imogen. Completely mundane. And suddenly I was tied to someone—tied in ways I couldn't see or understand, feeling emotions that weren't mine, unable to leave without his permission because the magic literally wouldn't let me."

Frost had stopped writing. His pen hovered over the page, his expression carefully controlled, but I saw the tension in his jaw.

"When did the abuse begin?"

Clara flinched at the word. "It wasn't—he didn't hit me. Not at first. It was subtler than that. He'd tell me what to wear, who to speak to, what to think. And when I disagreed, I'd feel this... wrongness. Like the bond itself was punishing me for disobedience. He called it 'correction.' Said I needed to learn how things worked in his world."

She set down her tea with a clatter, liquid sloshing over the rim.

"The scars came later. When I tried to run the first time. He said he needed to 'anchor' me more securely. He hired a Scribe—someone I never saw clearly, someone who came in the night—and they did something to the bond. Made it tighter. Made it hurt when I even thought about leaving."

My blood ran cold. "A Scribe modified your marriage bond without consent."

"Yes."

"Do you remember anything about them? Voice, build, mannerisms?"

"Male. Soft-spoken. He called Eli 'cousin,' I think, but that might have been a figure of speech." She wrapped her arms around herself. "He had tools. Silver things that looked like surgical instruments. He said the modifications would make me 'more comfortable' in my role."

Frost and I exchanged a look. Silver instruments. Bond modification. A Scribe who called Elias Thorne "cousin."

"The Vane family has marriage connections to the Thornes," Frost said quietly. "Julian Vane would be Elias's second cousin."

"Julian was at the warehouse," I said. "But he was using artifacts, not Scribe techniques. If there's another Vane involved—"

"Julian." Clara's voice was barely a whisper. "The Scribe's name was Julian. I heard Eli say it once, when he didn't know I was listening."

Julian Vane.

The name landed like a stone in still water. Not Julian—the hired muscle, the reality-bender we'd captured at the warehouse. Julian. Someone with actual Scribe abilities. Someone who could modify bonds, harvest power, create the kind of precise magical architecture we'd seen in the workshop.

Someone who was still out there.

"Clara." I kept my voice steady. "How did you escape?"

She was quiet for a long moment. When she spoke, her voice was distant, remembering.

"Three years ago. Eli had a business meeting—something important, he said. He'd be gone overnight. I'd been planning for months, saving small amounts of money, researching how to disappear. I knew the bond would hurt when I left. I didn't know how much."

Her hand moved to her forearm, rubbing the sleeve where I knew the scars lay hidden.

"I walked out the front door at midnight. The bond... screamed. It felt like being torn apart from the inside. I collapsed in the street two blocks away. A woman found me—an elderly woman walking her dog. She called an ambulance. The mundane doctors couldn't explain my injuries. Internal bleeding without trauma. Nerve damage without cause."

"Bond severance shock," I said. "The magic trying to drag you back."

"I should have died. The doctors said I should have died. But I didn't. And when I woke up three days later, the bond was..." She paused, searching for words. "Stretched. Thin. Like a thread pulled to its breaking point. It hurt constantly, but it couldn't control me anymore. Couldn't compel me back to him."

"You damaged the bond by forcing physical distance beyond its tolerance threshold," Frost said. His voice held something I hadn't heard before—a kind of grim respect. "That shouldn't be survivable."

"I'm stubborn." Clara's smile was wan. "Ask Imogen."

"She's the most stubborn person I know," I confirmed. "Present company excepted."

Frost's mouth twitched.

"I spent six months recovering," Clara continued. "Changed my name. Moved to the other side of London. Found work that didn't require magical background checks. And then I found Imogen's office, and I saw what she did for people like me, and I thought... maybe I could help. Maybe I could do something useful with what I'd survived."

"You never told me," I said quietly.

"I couldn't. The bond was still there—faint, but there. If I talked about Eli, if I even thought about him too much, it would pulse. Remind me he was still connected to me." She met my eyes. "When I heard he was dead, I felt it snap. Like a guitar string breaking. For the first time in four years, I was completely free."

"That's why you were upset when I came home," I realised. "Not just worry about me. Relief. Guilt about feeling relieved."

"He was murdered," Clara said. "And part of me was glad. What kind of person does that make me?"

"A survivor," Frost said. The word carried weight. "You endured systematic magical abuse, escaped against impossible odds, rebuilt your life from nothing. Your relief at his death is not a moral failing. It's a natural response to the end of your imprisonment."

Clara stared at him. "That's... not what I expected you to say."

"I've seen what people do to each other in the name of love and family and tradition." Frost closed his notebook with quiet finality. "I've stopped expecting victims to feel the emotions society tells them they should."

The room was silent for a moment. Something passed between them—recognition, perhaps. The acknowledgment of wounds that couldn't be seen.

"The Scribe," I said, pulling us back to the investigation. "Julian Vane. Did you ever see him again after the modification?"

"No. But Eli talked about him sometimes. Called him his 'consultant.' Said Julian was helping him with 'investments' that would make them both very wealthy."

"What kind of investments?"

"I don't know exactly. But Eli was obsessed with what he called 'Soul Equity.' He said the old families were sitting on fortunes they didn't even understand—power locked up in marriage bonds and blood oaths, just waiting to be liquidated." Clara shivered. "I thought he was speaking metaphorically. Now I'm not sure."

Soul Equity. The same term from Grimsby's research. The same concept Miller had found in Julian Vane's financial records.

"The Thorne marriage represented significant magical investment," Frost said slowly. "Ancient bloodlines on both sides. If someone were harvesting power from high-value bonds—"

"Elias would have been a target," I finished. "Not just a victim. An asset."

"Which means whoever killed him wasn't an enemy," Clara said, understanding dawning. "They were a business partner. Collecting on an investment."

The pieces clicked together with horrible precision.

Julian Vane. A Scribe with the knowledge to modify bonds, to harvest power, to create the kind of systematic extraction operation Grimsby had documented. Working with his cousin Julian, who provided the muscle and the Border Realm access. Targeting wealthy marriages, severing the bonds, collecting the magical energy for some larger purpose.

And Clara had been married to one of their early experiments. Had survived the modification process. Had escaped before they could harvest her husband's bond.

"Clara." I gripped her hands tightly. "When you escaped, was your bond to Elias intact?"

"I... I told you. It was stretched. Damaged. But still there."

"Still there. Still connecting you to him. Still representing magical investment that someone might want to collect."

Her face went pale. "You think they know about me?"

"I think Elias Thorne's marriage bond was severed three days ago. And I think whoever did it would have noticed that the bond was already damaged—that it led somewhere other than his wife's body." I looked at Frost. "They'll trace it. They'll find her."

"We don't know that," Frost said, but his voice lacked conviction.

"Julian Vane modified her bond personally. He knows she exists. He knows she escaped. And now that Elias is dead, she's a loose end—a witness who can identify him, connect him to the modifications, testify about his involvement."

Clara had started shaking again. "I can't—I can't go back to that. I can't—"

"You won't." I pulled her into my arms, holding her the way she'd held me after nightmares, after bad cases, after the weight of everything threatened to crush us both. "I won't let them touch you. Neither will Nathaniel."

The use of his first name was deliberate. I felt Frost's attention sharpen, felt the implicit promise I was making on his behalf.

"Miss Blackwell is correct," he said after a moment. "You will be placed under protective surveillance. My personal guarantee."

Clara laughed—a broken, desperate sound. "The M.O.P. protecting me from the system they're part of. That's rich."

"I'm not the M.O.P. tonight." Frost stood, moving toward the door. "Tonight I'm a man whose family may have enabled your suffering. Whose institution failed to protect you when protection was needed. I cannot undo what was done to you. But I can ensure it doesn't happen again."

He paused at the threshold, looking back at us—two women huddled together on a narrow bed, surrounded by the evidence of lives rebuilt from wreckage.

"I'll station officers outside the building," he said. "Discreet. Unmarked. If anyone approaches who shouldn't, they'll be intercepted."

"And Julian Vane?"

"We have Julian in custody. He'll talk eventually. When he does, we'll find his cousin." Frost's grey eyes were cold now, the vulnerability of earlier buried beneath something harder. "And then we'll end this."

He left without waiting for a response. I heard him speaking quietly to Pip in the other room, heard the front door open and close.

Clara and I sat in silence.

"I'm sorry," she said finally. "I should have told you. From the beginning. I should have—"

"You survived," I cut her off. "You did what you had to do to survive. That's nothing to apologise for."

"But if I'd told you, you might have seen the connection earlier. You might have—"

"Clara." I pulled back, cupping her face in my hands the way I had earlier. "Listen to me. None of this is your fault. Not Elias, not the bond, not the investigation. You are a victim of a system designed to exploit people exactly like you. The only people responsible are the ones who built that system and the ones who are now harvesting it."

She closed her eyes. Tears slipped down her cheeks.

"I'm scared," she whispered.

"I know."

"I don't want to go back to being that person. The one who couldn't leave, couldn't think, couldn't breathe without permission."

"You won't. You're not her anymore." I wiped her tears with my thumbs. "You're Clara Vance. My business partner. My friend. The most stubborn, most generous, most infuriatingly optimistic person I've ever known. And whoever Julian Vane thinks he is, he's never faced anyone like us."

She laughed again—still broken, but warmer now. "Us against the entire corrupt magical establishment. Those seem like fair odds."

"We've beaten worse."

"We've never faced worse."

"Then it's about time we did."

I helped her lie down, pulled the blankets up to her chin, sat beside her until her breathing steadied and her eyes closed. When I was certain she was asleep—or at least resting—I slipped out and closed the door quietly behind me.

Pip waited in the hallway, his small face unusually solemn.

"Inspector Frost has deployed surveillance assets," he reported. "Two officers in an unmarked vehicle across the street. Two more covering the rear entrance. Ward-stones placed at all threshold points."

"Good."

"He also left instructions that you should sleep, Miss Blackwell. He emphasized the word 'should' with particular intensity, which I interpreted as an order he knew you would ignore."

Despite everything, I smiled. "He's learning."

"He is... not what I expected." Pip climbed onto my shoulder, settling into his familiar position. "His file requires significant revision. I may need to add additional categories."

"Such as?"

"Unexpected Emotional Complexity. Potential Trustworthiness Pending Further Observation. And—" He paused delicately. "Possible Romantic Entanglement Requiring Close Monitoring."

"Pip."

"I am merely noting observable data, Miss Blackwell. It is not my fault that the data is increasingly suggestive."

I carried him into the main room, where Grimsby's research still lay spread across my desk. The evidence of conspiracy and murder, the threads of an investigation that now reached into my own home, my own family.

Clara was connected to Elias Thorne.

Julian Vane had modified her bond.

And somewhere out there, a man who called himself a reformer was harvesting the wealth of magical society one murdered husband at a time.

I sat at my desk and began to read through Grimsby's notes again, searching for any mention of Julian Vane, any hint of what he might be building with all that stolen power.

The investigation wasn't just professional anymore.

It was personal.

And I would burn down every institution in super-natural London before I let them hurt Clara again.

Chapter 8: The Ledger of Debts

Sleep came in fragments, each one interrupted by the sound of Clara's voice describing silver instruments and midnight modifications.

I gave up around four in the morning and moved to the kitchen, where I made tea I didn't drink and stared at Grimsby's research notes until the words blurred into meaningless shapes. The radiator clanked its usual complaints. Outside, London shifted from black to grey, the flat grey of October mornings that promised nothing but more grey.

Pip found me there at half past six, still in yesterday's clothes, cold tea untouched beside a stack of papers covered in my own handwriting.

"You have not slept." He climbed onto the table, surveying the scattered documents with professional disapproval. "Your penmanship deteriorates significantly after midnight. These notes are barely legible."

"My penmanship is fine."

"Your penmanship suggests a woman in the grip of obsessive pattern-matching who has forgotten basic self-maintenance." He nudged my untouched teacup. "This is cold. Cold tea is an abomination. I will make fresh."

He hopped down and began the elaborate process of tea preparation, which for Pip involved climbing the counter, operating the kettle through a system of pulleys he'd installed himself, and providing running commentary on proper steeping times.

I let his voice wash over me while I stared at the name I'd written seventeen times across three pages.

Julian Vane.

Not Julian—the hired muscle, the reality-bender we'd captured at the warehouse. Julian. Someone with actual Scribe abilities. Someone who could modify bonds, harvest power, create the kind of precise magical architecture we'd seen in that underground workshop.

Someone who had touched Clara. Who had tightened chains she couldn't see until they became scars she couldn't hide.

"Miss Blackwell." Pip's voice cut through my spiral. He stood on the counter's edge, a fresh cup of tea steaming beside him. "You are making the face."

"What face?"

"The one that precedes inadvisable decisions. I have catalogued seven variations. This is Type Three: righteous fury masquerading as analytical focus." He pushed the tea toward me with both paws. "Drink. Think. Then act. In that order."

I took the cup. The warmth helped, grounding me in the present rather than the imagined future where I did something regrettable to Julian Vane's contract-writing hands.

"Clara's bond to Elias was never fully severed," I said, thinking aloud. "Stretched. Damaged. But still connected. Which means—"

"Which means when Elias Thorne's bonds were harvested three days ago, anyone examining the threads would have noticed an anomaly." Pip's ears flattened. "A connection leading somewhere unexpected."

"Leading to Clara."

"Julian Vane modified that bond personally. He knows it exists. He knows she escaped." Pip's amber eyes held mine. "And now that Elias is dead, she represents an unresolved investment. A loose thread in his ledger."

The kitchen felt smaller suddenly. The wards Frost had placed seemed inadequate against the weight of what we were discussing.

"He'll come for her."

"He will attempt to." Pip's voice carried an edge I rarely heard from him. "Whether he succeeds is another matter entirely."

Clara emerged from her room at eight, wrapped in a cardigan two sizes too large, her face carrying the worn look of someone who had slept but not rested. She moved to the kitchen without speaking, poured herself tea from the pot Pip had prepared, and sat across from me at the small table.

We didn't discuss the previous night. We didn't need to. The weight of it sat between us like a third presence, acknowledged but not addressed.

"Frost's officers are still outside," she said finally. "I saw them when I checked the window. Two in a car across the street, trying very hard to look like they're not watching our building."

"Two more at the rear entrance. Ward-stones at all threshold points."

"He's thorough."

"He's worried."

Clara wrapped both hands around her cup, absorbing its warmth. "About me? Or about what I know?"

"Both, I think." I pushed my scattered notes aside, creating space between us. "Clara, what you told us last night—about Julian, about the modifications—that information changes everything. You're not just a survivor anymore. You're a witness. The only person who can directly connect Julian Vane to bond manipulation."

"I know." Her voice was steady, but her hands trembled slightly against the ceramic. "I've been thinking about that all night. About what it means. About what he might do to prevent me from testifying."

"We won't let him."

"You can't promise that." She looked up, and I saw the old fear there—the fear that had lived in her eyes when she first came to me, contract in hand, asking if escape was possible. "You can't promise anything, Imogen. That's what I learned from my marriage. Promises are just words until someone has the power to enforce them."

I reached across the table and covered her hand with mine. Her skin was cold despite the tea.

"Then I won't promise. I'll just do."

She almost smiled. "That sounds like something Marcus would have said."

The mention of my mentor's name created a small ache beneath my ribs. Grimsby had died trying to expose systematic exploitation. Now his research sat on my kitchen table, and the same patterns he'd documented were threatening someone I loved.

"Grimsby was researching this," I said. "Years ago. He called it the Collector's Mark—a signature used by someone harvesting magical debts. He never finished the work. He died before he could."

"You think Julian killed him?"

"I think Grimsby got close to something. Close enough that someone decided he needed to be silenced." I squeezed her hand once, then released it.

"And I think Frost knows more than he's told me about why the case was closed."

A knock at the door made us both freeze.

Pip materialized on the table between us, ears pricked forward. "Inspector Frost. I recognise the clipped rhythm of bureaucratic impatience."

I rose and crossed to the door, checking through the small window before unlocking the bolt. Frost stood in the hallway in his customary charcoal suit, but something about his posture suggested he'd slept as poorly as I had. The lines around his eyes seemed deeper, and he held his pocket watch in one hand as though he'd forgotten to return it to his waistcoat.

"Miss Blackwell." He inclined his head. "I apologise for the early hour."

"It's hardly early for people who haven't slept." I stepped aside to let him enter. "Tea?"

"Please."

He moved into the flat with careful awareness, cataloguing details the way he had during his first visit—the worn furniture, the cluttered bookshelves, the stack of Grimsby's notes now joined by my own midnight scribblings. His gaze lingered on Clara, assessing, before he took the chair I gestured toward.

"Miss Vance. How are you feeling?"

Clara's laugh held little humour. "Like someone who spent the night remembering things she'd worked very hard to forget. But I imagine that's the expected response."

"There is no expected response to trauma." Frost set his pocket watch on the table beside him—the same gesture of disarmament I'd noticed before, setting aside his constant companion. "Only the response that happens. How you feel is how you feel."

Something flickered across Clara's face. Surprise, perhaps, at finding compassion beneath the inspector's formal exterior.

Pip served tea with his usual efficiency, providing Frost with a cup and then retreating to the filing cabinet to observe from a position of tactical advantage. The morning light had strengthened while we talked, casting long shadows across the kitchen floor.

For a moment, no one spoke. The radiator clanked. Clara cradled her tea. Frost held his cup with both hands, the bandaged fingers wrapped around the ceramic with a care that suggested the warmth mattered more than the drink.

I watched his hands and thought about last night.

Not the photograph. Not Clara's revelation, or the hours of testimony that had followed, or the terrible arithmetic of Julian Vane's predation assembling itself across my kitchen table.

Before that. The study. Grimsby's notes spread between us, and his bandaged fingers hovering near my cheek, and the way the flat had gone quiet around us as though the building itself had drawn a breath and held it.

I had leaned into his palm. I had chosen to close the distance rather than maintain it. That fact sat in my chest like an unsigned contract—present, consequential, demanding attention I refused to give it.

Frost's gaze met mine across the table. Held for exactly one beat too long. Then he looked down at his tea with the controlled precision of a man choosing not to see something.

Neither of us mentioned it. Of course we didn't. Between then and now, Clara's world had fractured, and the private architecture of whatever had almost happened in my study had been buried under the rubble. There were more important things. There were always more important things.

But I noticed—and was irritated at myself for noticing—that he had taken the chair farthest from mine. That his posture held a degree of additional rigidity, as though compensating for some structural weakness he didn't want examined. That when Clara passed between us to refill the teapot, he shifted his weight away from my side of the table with a movement so small it could only have been conscious.

He was being careful. The kind of careful that only mattered if something had changed.

Something had changed.

Clara, who missed nothing when it came to the emotional weather of a room, glanced between us with an expression I chose not to interpret. She said nothing. Small mercies.

I stood and crossed to the counter where Clara's stress-baking from the previous day had produced an improbable surplus of scones. I wrapped four in a clean cloth and set them beside Frost's elbow without comment.

He looked at the bundle. Then at me.

"You haven't eaten," I said. "Don't tell me you have, because you hold your cup with both hands when your blood sugar drops and you've been doing it since you walked in."

The observation came out more precisely than I'd intended—the kind of detail you only possessed if you'd been cataloguing someone's habits without meaning to. I heard it the moment it left my mouth, and I could feel Clara's attention sharpen from across the room like a blade being drawn.

Frost's expression did something I hadn't seen before. The careful control didn't crack—it softened. Just at the edges. Just enough that I could see the exhaustion he'd been holding at bay, and beneath it, something tentative and startled, as though being noticed was a thing that happened to other people.

"Thank you," he said. Quietly. Without the formal cadence that usually armoured the phrase.

He unwrapped a scone and ate it in silence. I returned to my chair and did not look at him. I looked at Grimsby's notes, at Clara's cold tea, at the grey October light pressing against the window. At anything, in fact, that was not the small, private expression that had just crossed Nathaniel Frost's face and which I was going to need a considerable amount of time to stop thinking about.

Pip's pen scratched against paper from his perch on the filing cabinet. I didn't look over, but I could feel the quality of his observation—pointed, satisfied, insufferable.

I would be hearing about this later. In triplicate.

"I've spent the night coordinating with Detective Inspector Miller," Frost said, accepting his tea with a nod of thanks. "He's been running background on Julian Vane through mundane channels. The results are... illuminating."

He withdrew a folder from inside his jacket—how he'd concealed something that size, I couldn't imagine—and spread several documents across the table.

"Vane maintains three separate bank accounts. One under his own name, clean and unremarkable. One under a shell company called 'Reformist Resources Limited.' One under his mother's maiden name, which receives regular deposits from the shell company and makes payments to luxury retailers, travel agencies, high-end establishments."

"Money laundering," I said.

"Mundane money laundering. Which gives Miller jurisdiction if we can prove the connection to magical crimes." Frost pointed to a column of figures, all in red. "But look at the overall pattern. Thirty thousand in overdraft across four accounts. Loans against three properties he doesn't actually own. Credit cards maxed. From a mundane perspective, this looks like standard fraud."

I studied the numbers, feeling the shape of something larger emerging from the data. "But it's not just mundane."

"No." Frost's grey eyes met mine. "He's using Soul Equity as collateral for loans he never intends to repay. The mundane debt is just surface evidence. U nderneath..." He paused, choosing his words. "Miller found payment records. Twelve different families over the past five years. Regular deposits labelled 'consulting fee' or 'advisory service.' All the victim families. He's charging them for the privilege of being defrauded."

Clara made a small sound—not quite a gasp, but close. "The families he's supposedly helping. The ones he advises on navigating magical society."

"Yes."

I pulled the documents closer, letting my mind work through the implications. The pattern was there, hidden in plain sight. Vane's reformist reputation, his advocacy for new-blood access, his carefully cultivated image as a helper of the vulnerable—all of it was cover. Infrastructure for something far more predatory.

"He borrows power from one family through contract loopholes," I said slowly, the shape becoming clearer. "Uses that borrowed power to make himself appear more magically impressive than he actually is. Leverages that false impression to marry into another family, gaining access to their Soul Equity through the marriage contract. Then..."

"Then he liquidates them," Frost finished. "To pay the debt to the first family."

"And when the first family wants their principal back, he moves to a third. Borrows from them to pay the first. Marries into a fourth to pay the third." I set down the documents, my hands steady despite the cold settling into my chest. "It's a Ponzi scheme. Constant motion preventing anyone from seeing the full picture. Treating magical bloodlines like assets in a failing hedge fund."

"The murders happen when the liquidity dries up," Frost said. "When someone asks for their return, or threatens to audit the books. He's not killing for pleasure or revenge. He's liquidating liabilities."

The kitchen felt very quiet. Outside, London continued its morning routine—traffic, pedestrians, the ordinary sounds of a city unaware of the predator operating within its magical underbelly.

Clara spoke first. "How many?"

Frost hesitated before answering. "Officer Green analysed his current client relationships this morning. Forty-three active advisory arrangements."

"Forty-three families." Clara's voice was barely a whisper. "Forty-three potential victims."

"Yes."

I stood, moving to the window, needing distance from the numbers and what they represented. The officers Frost had stationed were still there, pretending to read newspapers in their unmarked car. Ordinary-looking people doing extraordinary work.

"He's running out of time," I said without turning around. "Miller's financial analysis shows he needs to consolidate within the next two weeks or the whole structure collapses. His mundane debts are catastrophic, which means his magical obligations must be worse."

"Which means he'll act soon." Frost's chair scraped as he rose. "He needs one final marriage to liquidate. Someone with significant Soul Equity who he can drain completely."

I turned from the window. Frost stood by the table, his formal posture rigid, but something in his eyes suggested the calculation happening behind them.

"Someone he already has access to," I said. "Someone vulnerable. Someone who—"

"Someone whose bond to a previous victim was never properly severed." Frost's gaze moved to

Clara. "Someone who represents unfinished business."

The colour drained from Clara's face

"He's not just coming for me as a witness," she said. "He's coming for me as an investment. The bond he modified—the connection to Elias—it still represents magical value to him. Power he helped create. Power he considers his to collect."

"Yes." Frost's voice was carefully controlled. "Miller's analysis suggests you may be his intended final liquidation. The one that saves his failing scheme or buries him completely."

I watched Clara process this new horror—not just the threat of a predator, but the knowledge that she'd been marked as an asset, a number on a ledger, a resource to be harvested.

Then something shifted in her expression. The fear didn't disappear, but it hardened into something else. Something I recognised from two years ago, when she'd sat in my office with a contract that was killing her and asked if there was any way out.

"Good," she said.

Frost blinked. "I beg your pardon?"

"Good." Clara rose from her chair, shoulders straightening. "If he's targeting me, that means we know where he'll come. It means we can plan. It means instead of waiting for him to strike at some unknown victim, we can be ready."

"Miss Vance—"

"Don't." She held up one hand. "Don't tell me it's too dangerous. Don't tell me I should hide and let others handle this. I spent three years as someone's possession, and I will not spend the rest of my life running from men who think they own me."

Pip made a small sound of approval from his position on the filing cabinet.

I looked at Clara—really looked at her, seeing past the fear and the trauma to the steel underneath. The same steel that had carried her through that midnight escape, through the agony of a stretching bond, through two years of rebuilding herself from wreckage.

"She's right," I said.

Frost turned to me, one eyebrow raised.

"If Vane is planning to target Clara, that gives us an advantage. We know his timeline. We know his methodology. We know who he'll approach and roughly when." I moved back to the table, gathering the scattered documents. "The question is whether we can build a case strong enough to stop him before he makes his move."

"The High Council—" Frost began.

"The High Council won't authorise intervention based on financial analysis and circumstantial evidence. We need more. We need proof that connects Julian directly to the murders, not just to fraud." I looked at him steadily. "We need Grimsby's research."

"Your mentor's files."

"He was investigating the same patterns. The Collector's Mark. The systematic harvesting of magical debts. Something in his notes might provide the connection we're missing." I paused, weighing the cost of what I was about to say. "I'll share everything. All of it. But I need access to the M.O.P.'s resources in return. Your archives. Your forensic analysis. Whatever evidence was gathered when Grimsby died and the case was closed." I watched his expression, reading the calculation there—the institutional loyalty warring with something more personal.

"The Grimsby case was sealed by High Council order," he said finally. "Accessing those files without authorisation would be a serious breach of protocol."

"I know."

"It could end my career if discovered."

"I know."

"And you're asking me to do it anyway."

I held his gaze. "I'm asking you to help me finish what Grimsby started. To find the truth about who killed him and why. To stop Julian Vane from doing to Clara—and forty-three other families—what he's done to everyone else who got in his way."

The pocket watch sat on the table between us, its ticking the only sound in the quiet kitchen.

"Grimsby taught me that the law could protect people if wielded correctly," I continued. "That contract work wasn't just bureaucracy, but actual defence against exploitation. He was murdered for believing it. For getting close to exposing the people who profit from predatory magic."

"And you want to walk the same path." Frost's voice was soft. "Knowing where it led him."

"I want to walk it further. I want to reach the end he never got to see." I straightened, pulling my professional armour back into place. "Are you with me or not?"

Frost looked at the documents spread across the table. At Clara, standing with her arms crossed and her jaw set. At Pip, watching from his filing cabinet perch with ancient, knowing eyes. At me.

Then he reached for his pocket watch and returned it to his waistcoat with a decisive click.

"Tonight," he said. "Come to the Citadel after dark. I'll have the Grimsby files ready." He paused at the door, looking back. "And Miss Blackwell? Whatever we find, whatever it costs—I failed your mentor once. I will not fail you."

The door closed behind him. The bolt slid home with a sound that felt like a contract being sealed.

Clara let out a breath she'd been holding. "Well. That was..."

"Unexpected," Pip supplied from his perch. "I shall need to revise Inspector Frost's file again. The categories are becoming unmanageable."

I looked at Grimsby's notes, still scattered across the table. At Clara, who had survived horrors I could barely imagine and was now volunteering to face them again. At the grey London morning visible through the window, full of ordinary people living ordinary lives while predators moved unseen among them.

"We have work to do," I said. "And not much time to do it."

Clara nodded once, then moved toward the kitchen. "I'll make breakfast. You need to eat before you plan the downfall of a murderer."

"I don't have time for—"

"Imogen." She turned, and her expression was equal parts affection and exasperation. "You cannot defeat evil on an empty stomach. That's basic battlefield strategy."

Despite everything, I almost smiled.

Pip hopped down from the filing cabinet and began organizing the scattered documents into neat piles, muttering about proper archival procedures and the inadequacy of kitchen tables as research facilities.

Outside, the M.O.P. officers maintained their watch. Somewhere in London, Julian Vane was making his own plans, unaware that his intended victim had just become his most dangerous enemy.

The investigation was shifting. No longer reactive, scrambling to understand murders after they happened. Now we had a target. A timeline. A chance.

Forty-three families at risk. One woman willing to become bait. One inspector breaking rules he'd upheld for decades. And one Scribe with Thread Sight, a Null-Ink pen, and the research notes of a dead mentor who had died trying to expose this exact corruption.

The odds were terrible.

But they were better than yesterday's.

Chapter 9: The Archive and the Tribunal

The Citadel rose from Blackfriars like a fist of soot-stained granite, its bulk crushing the skyline into submission. I had visited twice before—once for my Scribe certification review, once to consult on a contract dispute that had involved minor assault charges. Neither visit had prepared me for approaching the building with purpose rather than obligation.

The October wind cut through my jacket as I climbed the front steps. Behind me, London continued its afternoon routine, oblivious to the architecture of magical authority looming over its mundane streets.

The entrance wards pressed against me as I crossed the threshold—not the honey-resistance of private homes, but something heavier. Active suppression designed to make visitors understand they had surrendered autonomy the moment they stepped inside. My Null status meant the magic couldn't bind me directly, but I still tasted copper and felt pressure building behind my eyes.

Frost waited in the entrance hall.

He stood beside the security desk with a leather case file held against his chest, both hands wrapped around it as though preventing escape. His charcoal suit was immaculate as always, but something about his posture suggested weight. The kind that accumulated when you were about to deliver news you'd been carrying for five years.

"Miss Blackwell." He inclined his head. "Thank you for coming."

"Inspector." I studied his face, reading tension in the set of his jaw, the careful way he held himself still. "You look like a man about to deliver bad news."

"The news is five years old." He gestured toward the corridor behind him. "We should speak privately."

I followed him through hallways painted institutional cream, past frosted glass doors bearing names in gold lettering. The building's atmosphere grew heavier with each floor we climbed—suppression wards layered over security protocols layered over centuries of bureaucratic authority. By the time we reached the third floor, my skin crawled with the accumulated weight of it.

The room Frost chose was small and windowless, iron filigree worked into the stone walls in patterns that made my eyes want to skip over them. An interrogation room, though he'd set it up for consultation—two chairs positioned across a metal table bolted to the floor, a carafe of water, two glasses.

He closed the door behind us. The sound of it latching felt like the end of something.

"Before we begin." Frost set the case file on the table between us but didn't open it. "I need you to understand what you're about to see. And why I didn't show you sooner."

I sat in one of the metal chairs, my document case balanced on my knees. "Go on."

"I investigated Marcus Grimsby's death five years ago." He remained standing, positioned near the door like a man who expected to need an exit. "The official report listed cause of death as ward failure—magical exhaustion from insufficient maintenance of his protective enchantments. That's what the archives say. That's what the public record shows."

"But?"

"But the evidence told a different story." Frost moved to the far wall, putting distance between us that felt deliberate. "Grimsby's wards were sophisticated, custom-designed, regularly updated. The kind of protections that don't fail without external interference. I found signs of intrusion—memory stone recordings from a neighbouring shop showing a figure in expensive clothing entering his building that evening. Glamour obscured facial features, but the gait suggested aristocratic training."

My hands flattened against my document case. "You're saying someone killed him."

"I'm saying his wards were breached from inside, suggesting he admitted his visitor willingly. I'm saying physical evidence from his office—his personal ward key, three contract ledgers, a locked steel box—was logged into M.O.P. archives and then transferred to High Council jurisdiction within a week of the investigation closing. No explanation. No authorisation signature. Just... gone."

The room felt smaller suddenly. The iron-worked walls pressed inward, and I understood why Frost had chosen this space. Containment. Privacy. Protection from ears that might be listening.

"Who ordered you to close the case?"

"Parties with sufficient political influence to ensure compliance." His voice remained flat, controlled. "I was advised that insufficient evidence existed to warrant continued resource expenditure. That pursuing conspiracy theories would damage department credibility. I was a junior inspector. I followed orders."

The carafe of water sat untouched between us. I stared at it rather than at Frost, processing implications that had been building for five years without my awareness.

"Grimsby was scheduled to testify before the High Council the week he died." I spoke slowly, fitting pieces together. "About systematic contract fraud targeting working-class supernatural beings."

"Forty-eight hours before his scheduled appearance. Yes."

"And the families implicated in his testimony?"

Frost opened the case file at last, spreading documents across the metal table with the precision of a man laying out evidence for trial. Crime scene photographs I'd never been permitted to see. Forensic analysis that contradicted the official report. Witness statements that were never formally entered into the record.

"Three families with Council connections. All with significant financial interests in maintaining the contract practises Grimsby planned to expose." He pointed to a specific document—a forensic diagram showing ward failure patterns. "Look at the degradation sequence. This wasn't brute force. This was administrative access. Someone who understood how to unravel permission structures rather than break through them."

I pulled the diagram closer, my Scribe training automatically analyzing the magical architecture. Grimsby had taught me this—how to read ward failures, how to identify the signature of different breaching techniques. What I saw made my stomach turn.

"Inverted anchor degradation." My finger traced the pattern. "They didn't attack his wards. They used legitimate access codes to deconstruct them from within. This is insider work."

"Yes."

"You knew this five years ago."

"I suspected." Frost's hands pressed flat against the table, mirroring my earlier position. "I couldn't prove it. The evidence had been moved. The witnesses had been made unavailable. And I was ordered to stop asking questions."

The photographs showed Grimsby's office as I'd never seen it—papers scattered, wards shattered into visible fragments like broken glass, his body collapsed at his desk. He looked peaceful in death, which was somehow worse than violence would have been. As if whoever killed him had taken care to pose him, to make the scene look like exhaustion rather than execution.

Grimsby had warned me once about binding sickness—what happened when too many violated oaths accumulated in a single practitioner. The magic turned cannibal, he'd said. Ate you from inside. I'd thought he was being theatrical. Looking at his photograph, I wondered if he'd been speaking from observation rather than theory.

I touched the edge of one photograph. The paper was cool against my fingertips.

"Why are you showing me this now?"

"Because the Vane scandal created an opening." Frost straightened, moving to the opposite side of the table. "Because the Council is divided in ways that make investigation possible when it wasn't before. And because..." He paused, choosing words with visible care. "Because I failed your mentor. I was ordered to stop, and I stopped. I told myself the system would self-correct, that justice would eventually prevail through proper channels. I was wrong. And I have spent five years knowing I was wrong while being unable to prove it."

"You could have told me sooner."

"I could have. I chose not to." He met my eyes directly. "You were building a practise. Helping people. Continuing his work in your own way. I didn't want to burden you with knowledge that would make you a target the way it made him a target."

"You don't get to make that choice for me."

"No. I don't." He inclined his head—acknowledgment, not apology. "Which is why I'm telling you now. The same patterns Grimsby documented are active in the current murders. The same families he planned to implicate have connections to Julian Vane's network. And the same people who ordered his case closed will almost certainly try to close this one when they realise what we're finding."

I stood, needing movement, needing space that the small room couldn't provide. Three steps toward the wall, turn, three steps back. The iron filigree hummed faintly against my awareness—suppression magic designed to contain rather than protect.

I was building a case. The recognition surfaced with uncomfortable clarity. Not reviewing contracts, not filing motions, not preparing analysis for someone else to argue before the Council. I was constructing a prosecution—identifying perpetrators, connecting evidence, forming the legal architecture of a trial strategy. Solicitor's work ended at the desk. What I was doing now was advocacy, and the Ethics Committee had a specific term for practising it without certification.

I pushed the thought aside. Terminology was a luxury for people whose mentors hadn't been murdered.

"I am in the exact position that killed him."

The words came out before I could stop them. Raw truth in a room designed for careful lies.

"I hold the same evidence," I continued, my voice sounding strange in my own ears. "I serve the same clients. I'm threatening the same interests. They didn't kill him for the crime of being Marcus Grimsby. They killed him for the crime of being inconvenient."

I turned to face Frost.

"And I have just made myself very inconvenient."

He crossed the room in three strides—not pacing, but moving with the lethal fluidity of a man who had decided something. He stopped two feet from me, close enough that I could feel the cold radiating from his skin, the constant chill that lived beneath his careful control.

"That outcome requires them to believe they can act with impunity." His voice had changed, the measured bureaucratic tone replaced by something harder. "They believe they are hunting a stray Scribe. They do not know they are hunting *us*."

"You cannot promise my safety."

"No." He held my gaze. "I can promise that if I must choose between the law and justice, I will choose justice. If I must choose between institutional authority and protecting the people that authority was supposed to serve, I will choose the people. And if anyone attempts to silence you the way they silenced Grimsby—" His jaw tightened. "I will ensure they understand the cost of that choice."

The iron-worked walls pressed inward. London existed somewhere beyond this room, mundane and magical, layered and hidden. But in this moment, the only reality was two people standing in a containment cell, deciding whether to trust each other with their lives.

"We need to present this evidence to the High Council," I said. "Formally. On the record."

"The Tribunal convenes this afternoon. I've requested an emergency session."

"They'll try to suppress it."

"They'll fail." Frost gathered the case file documents with precise movements, organizing evidence into the order of presentation. "The reform faction has enough votes to force a hearing. Baroness Ashford's family was touched by Vane's scheme—she has personal motivation to see this through. And once evidence enters the formal record, it can't be quietly transferred to restricted archives. Too many witnesses."

"You've been planning this."

"I've been preparing for the possibility." He met my eyes again. "Since the moment I realised the current murders connected to Grimsby's research. The question was whether you would want to pursue it, knowing the risks."

I thought of Clara, sleeping in our flat under M.O .P. protection. Of Pip, organizing files with ferocious determination. Of forty-three families who had no idea they were marked for liquidation by a man they trusted.

"Show me the Tribunal chamber," I said.

The Tribunal took three hours.

Frost presented evidence with the methodical precision I'd come to expect—financial analysis, contract patterns, the connection to Grimsby's death. I stood in the salt circle and answered Augusta's questions with professional neutrality that felt increasingly like armour. Clara testified briefly, quietly, without wavering. Several Council members shifted uncomfortably as she described what had been done to her.

The verdict was a partial win, as institutional verdicts always are.

Fourteen days of authorised investigation. Provisional consultant status for me. A refusal to formally reopen Grimsby's case, tempered by an acknowledgment of "irregularities in original case handling"—political language for *we know something was wrong and we're not ready to say* so *publicly*.

Augusta's final warning carried the weight of centuries: pursue justice through evidence, not agenda, or face consequences.

Standing outside the Old Bailey afterward, October wind cutting through my jacket, I thought of Grimsby preparing to testify in that same chamber five years ago. He had died the night before his testimony. I had got further than he had.

Whether that would be enough remained to be seen.

"Fourteen days," Clara said beside me. "Is that enough?"

"It will have to be."

Frost checked his pocket watch—the ritual gesture I'd come to recognise as his anchor, his constant. "I have officers monitoring Vane's known locations. If he moves, we'll know."

"He'll move." I looked at the city beyond—grey sky, grey stone, grey people moving through their grey lives unaware of predators in their midst. "His financial structure is collapsing. Clara represents his best chance at stabilization. He'll come for her."

"Then we'll be ready."

We walked into October afternoon, three people and one brownie against a conspiracy that had operated unchecked for fifteen years. The odds were still terrible. But for the first time since Grimsby died, I had authorisation to pursue justice rather than just dream of it.

Somewhere in London, Julian Vane was making plans. So were we.

Chapter 10: The Trap Already Set

The flat smelled of perfume and possibility when I climbed the stairs that evening.

I had spent the afternoon at the Citadel, coordinating with Frost's team on surveillance priorities. Fourteen days of authorisation. Forty-three families at risk. One target who had eluded detection for fifteen years. The mathematics of the situation pressed against my temples like an approaching headache.

Clara's door stood open. Light spilled into the hallway, accompanied by humming I didn't recognise—something bright and hopeful that made my chest tighten with premonition.

I set my document case down and hung my coat on its hook. Every movement felt weighted, as if the day's revelations had added physical mass to my bones.

"Imogen!" Clara's voice carried from her bedroom, warm with excitement. "Perfect timing. Which one?"

I appeared in her doorway to find her holding two cardigans against a cream-coloured dress laid across the bed. She glowed. There was no other word for it. Her strawberry blonde hair fell in careful curls, her makeup subtle but enhancing, her whole bearing transformed by something I hadn't seen in her for years.

Hope.

"The lavender," I said, managing something resembling a smile. "It brings out your eyes."

"That's what I thought." She tossed the pink cardigan onto her vanity chair—already cluttered with cosmetics and jewellery—and turned back to her mirror. "I met someone. Last week, at that gallery opening. Remember? The one with the terrible modern sculpture?"

I remembered. I'd spent most of the evening analyzing a property contract in the corner while Clara mingled, grateful that she was willing to attend social functions I found exhausting.

"He's wonderful, Imogen. Really wonderful." Clara applied mascara with careful strokes, her eyes bright in the mirror's reflection. "Charming, witty, genuinely interested in what I think. Not just..." She paused, the brush hovering. "You know. What I used to be able to do."

The words landed with their usual weight. Clara rarely mentioned her crippled magic directly, preferring euphemism and implication. That she mentioned it now, in the context of this new person, suggested something significant.

I leaned against the doorframe, fighting the exhaustion that wanted to drag me toward tea and unconsciousness. "What's he like?"

"Sandy blonde. A regular at the theater. Well-connected, but he doesn't name-drop." She set down the mascara and met my eyes in the mirror. "Last week he spent twenty minutes discussing whether Blake's illustrations were better than his poetry, and he actually listened when I disagreed. He makes me feel seen. As a person. Not as broken. Not as damage."

The details assembled themselves in my mind with the precision of contract clauses clicking into place. Sandy blonde. Theater regular. Charming. Connected. Someone who made vulnerable women feel seen and valued.

The pattern resolved into a single, terrible name.

"Clara." My voice came out strange, stripped of its usual professional cadence. "What is his name?"

"Julian Vane." She smiled at her reflection, checking her lipstick. "He's a reformer. Works with families transitioning into magical society. Helps them navigate without getting exploited by predatory contracts."

The world narrowed to that name in Clara's mouth.

I crossed the room in three steps and stood behind her chair. Our eyes met in the vanity mirror—hers bright with anticipation, mine gone flat with horror.

"You cannot see him."

The command hung in the air, stripping the warmth from the room like frost killing flowers. Clara's smile faltered, then vanished.

"What?"

"Julian Vane is not a suitor." The words came out too sharp, too fast. I forced my voice down, tried to find the careful professional tone that had served me through a thousand difficult conversations. "He is the subject of our investigation. The one we just received authorisation to pursue. He targets vulnerable people, leverages their trust, and liquidates them when they become inconvenient. He has killed at least four people, Clara. Possibly more. You cannot go on this date."

She set down her lipstick with deliberate care. The small click of plastic against wood was the only sound in the suddenly quiet room.

"Are you certain?"

"Marriage contracts modified to include soul-equity clauses. All victims connected to Vane as financial advisor. He's running a Ponzi scheme using magical bloodlines as collateral, and he murders people when they get too close to discovering the fraud." I gripped the back of her chair, knuckles whitening. "He approached you because you're connected to me. Because you're vulnerable. Because targeting you sends me a message."

Clara stood. We were nearly the same height—she had perhaps an inch on me—but in this moment she seemed to tower, her spine straightening with an anger I'd rarely seen from her.

"You're forbidding me from seeing someone because he might be dangerous." Her voice shook. "Do you know how that sounds? How many times I've heard those exact words?"

"This isn't about control—"

"It's exactly about control." She stepped away from the vanity, putting distance between us. "I spent three years trapped in a marriage where someone made every decision for me. Controlled every aspect of my life. Told me who I could see, what I could think, how I should feel. And now you're standing in my bedroom, forbidding me from going on a date because you've decided you know better."

"Because I do know better." The words came out harder than I intended. "I've seen his pattern, Clara. I've read his contracts. I know exactly what men like Julian Vane do to women like you."

"Women like me." She repeated the phrase flatly. "What does that mean, exactly? Damaged? Desperate? Willing to ignore warning signs because someone charming is paying attention?"

The accuracy of the accusation stole my breath.

"That's not—"

"That's exactly what you meant." Clara moved toward the wardrobe where the lavender cardigan hung. I shifted without thinking, blocking her path.

Wrong move. I knew it the moment I did it.

"Get out of my way." Her voice dropped, quiet and dangerous.

"Clara, please. Just postpone the date. Give Frost time to investigate. If I'm wrong—"

"You're not wrong about Vane." She met my eyes directly. "You're probably right. He probably is exactly what you say he is. But that doesn't give you the right to make this decision for me."

"He will kill you."

"You don't know that."

"I do. I've seen the pattern. I've read the contracts. I know—"

"You know what's in documents." Clara's hands clenched at her sides. "You don't know what it's like to spend five years feeling like something less than human. To wake up every morning and remember what you used to be able to do. To look in every mirror and see scars instead of skin. To wonder, every time someone looks at you, whether they see a person or just... damage."

Her voice cracked on the last word.

"I see a person," I said. "I have always seen a person."

"You see someone who needs protecting." She stepped past me—I didn't try to stop her this time—and grabbed the cardigan from its hanger. "Julian sees someone whole. And I'm going to find out if that's real or not, because I would rather take the risk than spend another five years too terrified to live."

"Even if the risk is your life?"

"My life. My choice." She turned to face me, purse clutched against her chest like armour. "You of all people should understand that. How many times have you taken risks for your clients? How many times have you walked into dangerous situations because you decided the potential outcome was worth the potential cost?"

"That's different."

"Why? Because you're the one making the calculation? Because your judgment is trustworthy and mine isn't?" Her laugh held no humour. "Everything is strategy with you, Imogen. Every relationship is a transaction. Every kindness is manipulation. You've spent so long refusing to let anyone close that you've forgotten what actual connection looks like."

The accusation landed. I felt it hit, felt the truth underneath the anger, felt shame, or maybe grief, I couldn't separate them.

"Clara." I kept my voice level through effort that felt physical. "I am asking you. Not commanding. Asking. Please don't go."

She studied my face for a long moment. Something softened in her expression—not enough to change her mind, but enough to acknowledge the fear underneath my demand.

"I know you're trying to protect me," she said quietly. "I know you mean well. But I have spent too long being protected from my own choices. I need to make my own mistakes. Even if they're catastrophic. Even if you're right about everything."

She moved toward the door.

"At least tell me where you're going."

"No." She paused at the threshold, looking back. "Because you'll send someone to watch. To intervene. To protect me from myself whether I want it or not."

"Clara—"

"I'll be home by eleven." She tried to smile. "If I'm not, you can worry then."

The front door opened and closed.

I stood in her empty bedroom, surrounded by discarded cardigans and scattered cosmetics and the lingering scent of her perfume. The radiator clanked. Outside, London continued its evening routine, oblivious to the trap closing around someone I loved.

The telephone sat on its small table in the hallway. I stared at it for a full minute before picking up the receiver and dialing the Citadel with fingers that wanted to shake.

Three rings.

"Metropolitan Occult Police, Blackfriars Citadel." Halloway's voice, gruff and efficient.

"Inspector Frost. Immediately."

"Who's calling?"

"Imogen Blackwell. It's urgent."

A pause. Muffled conversation. Then Frost's voice, controlled and precise.

"Miss Blackwell. What's happened?"

"Julian Vane has made contact with Clara." The words came out clipped and professional, the only way I could make them come out at all. "My flatmate. They have a date tonight. He approached her last week at a gallery opening. She doesn't believe he's dangerous."

I heard Frost processing, calculating, adjusting.

"Where are they meeting?"

"I don't know. She didn't say. She left approximately three minutes ago."

"Can you reach her? Contact her before the meeting?"

"She won't answer." I pressed my free hand against the table edge, grounding myself. "She believes I'm being overprotective. That I'm projecting my fears rather than responding to genuine danger."

"Are you?"

The question was fair. I hated it anyway.

"He's targeting her to get to me. To demonstrate that he can reach anyone I care about. This entire courtship is theater, designed to show me that I can't protect the people I love."

"Yes." Frost's agreement was immediate. "That would be consistent with his pattern. Hold on."

More muffled conversation. I heard him giving orders—location traces, surveillance teams, coordination protocols. When he returned, his voice had shifted slightly. Still controlled, but with an edge underneath.

"We'll track her mobile phone. Find the restaurant. Deploy surveillance." A pause. "Miss Blackwell. I need you to remain at your flat in case Miss Vance returns early or attempts to contact you."

"No."

"This is not negotiable."

"You're correct. It's not." I straightened, though he couldn't see me. "Clara is my responsibility. I'm not sitting here while Vane—"

"While Vane takes her to dinner in a public location where harming her would expose him to dozens of witnesses?" Frost's tone remained level. "He won't hurt her tonight. This is reconnaissance. Establishing connection. Building trust before the trap closes. Having you rush to the location will worsen the situation. If Miss Vance sees you, it confirms her belief that you're overreacting. It pushes her closer to Vane, who will position himself as the reasonable one. The one who respects her choices."

His logic was cold, accurate, and entirely unhelpful.

"How long?"

"Thirty minutes to establish her location. Another thirty to deploy surveillance. I'll contact you as soon as we have visual confirmation that she's safe."

The line went dead before I could argue further.

I stood in the hallway, receiver still pressed to my ear, listening to silence.

Frost sent a car for me at half past eight.

Halloway drove without speaking, navigating through evening traffic with professional efficiency. I sat in the back seat, watching London slide past the windows—ordinary people living ordinary lives, unaware of predators moving among them.

The restaurant was in Mayfair. The Silver Room, according to the sign—a name I recognised from society gossip, the sort of establishment where reservations required connections and meals cost more than my monthly heating bill. Candlelight glowed behind tall windows. Well-dressed couples visible through the glass.

Frost waited in a doorway across the street, positioned where shadows pooled between streetlamps. Duan patrolled the pavement with studied casualness, appearing to window-shop at a closed boutique. Green sat in a parked van fifty meters away, equipment humming as she monitored the restaurant's ward signatures.

"Visual confirmation," Frost said as I approached. "Miss Vance and Vane arrived forty minutes ago. Corner table near the back. Private but visible."

"Has he—"

"Nothing unusual. Standard dinner service. He's been attentive but appropriate. No signs of magical interference."

I moved to stand beside him in the doorway, my coat inadequate against the October chill. Through the restaurant's windows, I could see golden light, elegant patrons, white tablecloths and silver service. But not Clara. Not from this angle.

"The High Council declined to authorise intervention," Frost continued. "Insufficient evidence of immediate threat. Political concerns regarding harassment of a prominent reformer."

"She's bait in a trap and they're worried about politics."

"Yes."

At least he didn't pretend otherwise.

The minutes crawled. I watched the restaurant's entrance, counting patrons entering and exiting, none of them Clara. Green's van hummed with electronic surveillance. Duan completed another circuit of her patrol route. Frost checked his pocket watch—the ritual gesture that had become as familiar as breathing—and returned it to his waistcoat without comment.

The doorway was narrow. Built for one, occupied by two. His shoulder sat six inches from mine, and I was aware of every one of those inches the way a cartographer is aware of the distance between coastlines—precisely, involuntarily, with a specificity that served no practical purpose.

The October cold pressed in from the street, but the air between us held a different temperature. Not warm—Nathaniel was never warm, his magic ran too close to the surface for that—but present. A boundary of cooled air that carried the wafting scent of warding stones and wool and something underneath that was simply him, clean and cold and faintly metallic, like frost on iron.

I had been standing next to him for nine minutes. I knew this because I had counted. Counting was preferable to the alternative, which was thinking about the courthouse steps three days ago and the way he'd said *she would have understood what you did in there* and the three seconds I'd allowed his name to exist uncorrected in my mind.

Thread Sight had been active since we'd arrived—necessary for monitoring the restaurant's ward signatures, for watching the magical architecture of the evening in case Vane attempted anything beyond a dinner reservation. Professional requirement. Entirely justified.

I should not have looked at Nathaniel.

I had looked at hundreds of people through Thread Sight. Thousands, probably, over the years of my practise. Every client who walked through my door, every opposing counsel in Tribunal, every stranger on the Tube whose threads happened to catch my eye. The magical connections that bound people to obligations, relationships, debts, and duties were as visible to me as the colour of their coats. I had long since learned to skim them the way a literate person skims headlines—registering, categorizing, moving on.

Nathaniel's threads were something I had never seen before.

I had expected complexity. His duty threads alone should have been a thicket—the Ashwood seal, the M.O.P., his family obligations, the Council authority he'd spent decades serving. And they were present, yes: silver-blue filaments radiating from his chest like the spokes of a wheel, some thick as rope (the seal, anchoring him always, the thread that made his pocket watch skip when the wards weakened), others fine as spider silk (professional courtesies, minor obligations, the accumulated architecture of a life spent in service).

But between those duty threads, woven through them with the delicacy of something that had grown rather than been constructed, I saw others.

A thread the colour of warm amber, running from somewhere near his sternum to the general direction of our flat. Clara. He had formed a protection bond with her—not contractual, not magical in the formal sense, but real. The kind of thread that appeared when someone decided, consciously or not, that another person's safety mattered to them. It was recent. Weeks old at most.

Beside it, thinner, a thread of brownie-gold that could only be Pip. Fainter, but present. Nathaniel Frost had somehow developed a connection to a fourteen-inch brownie who kept files on him cross-referenced by probability of betrayal.

And there—

I stopped looking.

I should have stopped looking. I meant to stop looking. My professional ethics, my training, every principle Grimsby had instilled in me about the sanctity of a person's private magical architecture demanded that I stop looking the moment I realised what I was seeing.

But Thread Sight doesn't pause for ethics. It shows you the whole picture and leaves the responsibility of looking away to your conscience. And my conscience, it seemed, was three seconds too slow.

The thread ran from his chest to mine.

It was new. Gossamer-thin, barely there, the magical equivalent of a pencil line drawn so faintly it might be mistaken for a shadow. Not a contract. Not a bond in any formal sense. Not something either of us had agreed to or signed or spoken into existence.

Just a connection. Forming the way connections form—through proximity and shared purpose and late nights over evidence and the accumulated weight of small truths exchanged on courthouse steps. Through scones delivered without comment and names allowed to linger three seconds in private thought and the gentle intimacy of standing in a doorway together, watching someone you both love walk into danger.

It was the colour of winter light through glass. Pale. Almost colourless. The kind of thread that might strengthen into something permanent or dissolve by morning depending on what the people at either end decided to do about it.

I looked away.

The restaurant's windows glowed. Clara was inside, invisible from this angle. Green's van hummed. Duan completed her patrol circuit. The ordinary machinery of surveillance continued exactly as before.

Frost hadn't moved. He couldn't know what I'd seen—Thread Sight was my ability, not his, and the threads I'd observed were visible only to Scribes. Reading someone's involuntary connections without their knowledge or consent violated Section Twelve of the Scribe Guild's Code of Professional Conduct. Grimsby had dedicated an entire month of my training to the ethics of unsolicited thread observation. *You will see things people don't know they're feeling*, he'd said. *That knowledge is not yours to use. It's barely yours to have.*

I pressed my spectacles higher on my nose. The gesture provided no help, but the familiarity of it steadied me.

The thread existed. It was real. It was mutual—I knew that with the clinical certainty of someone trained to read magical architecture, because threads of that kind only formed between two points of origin, never one.

Which meant that whatever I was refusing to feel, he was refusing to feel it too. And neither of us had agreed to this. Neither of us had signed anything or spoken anything or made any conscious choice to allow it. It had simply grown, the way moss grows on stone—slowly, in the spaces between attention, fed by conditions neither party had created on purpose.

I was going to need a very long time to think about this. Preferably alone. Preferably with tea. Preferably without a fourteen-inch brownie demanding to update his files.

For now, I folded the knowledge into the most private compartment of my mind and locked it there with the same care I used to seal client confidences. Some information was too consequential to act on in a doorway in Mayfair while Clara's life hung in the balance.

Some information changed everything, and therefore had to change nothing. Not yet.

I shifted my weight a fraction to the left, increasing the distance between our shoulders from six inches to eight.

Frost glanced at me. I kept my eyes on the restaurant.

Nine o'clock became nine-thirty. Nine-thirty crawled toward ten.

"Miss Blackwell." Frost's voice was quiet. "You should know that whatever happens tonight, we will protect her. This is one date. One evening. Vane won't move against her immediately—his pattern requires extended grooming, the establishment of emotional dependency. We have time."

"Do we?" I kept my eyes on the restaurant. "He knows we're investigating him. He knows he's running out of options. What if he accelerates the timeline?"

"Then we accelerate ours."

"And if that's not fast enough?"

He didn't answer. We both knew there was no good answer.

The restaurant door opened.

Clara emerged, Vane beside her. She was laughing—head tilted back, genuine delight in the sound. He helped her with her coat, solicitous and attentive, the perfect picture of courtly attention.

My hands clenched at my sides.

Vane raised his hand. A black cab materialized from traffic, pulling to the curb with the precision of a summoned servant. He opened the door for Clara, handed her into the back seat, leaned through the window.

They kissed.

Brief. Chaste. Appropriate for a first date in public view.

Clara was glowing.

The cab pulled away. Vane stood on the pavement, watching it disappear down the street. Then he turned.

And looked directly at where we stood.

The distance was too great for casual observation. The shadows too deep for any natural line of sight. But his gaze found us anyway—found me—with the precision of a blade finding its mark.

He smiled.

It was a small expression, carefully calibrated. A social gesture weaponized into threat. He raised his hand in a small wave, the movement unhurried and exact, as if acknowledging an acquaintance across a crowded room. As if we were old friends. As if he wanted me to understand, with perfect clarity, that he had known we were watching the entire time.

Then he turned and walked away, hands in his pockets, perfectly relaxed.

"He knew." Duan's voice came from my left. She'd moved closer during the exit. "He knew we were here."

"Yes." Frost's hand touched my shoulder briefly—restraining, grounding. "Let him go."

"He just—"

"Demonstrated that Miss Vance is accessible. That he can touch her life whenever he chooses." Frost's voice remained controlled, but something underneath it wasn't. "This entire evening was theater. For your benefit."

I watched the corner where Vane had disappeared, my heart beating a rhythm of helpless rage.

Green emerged from her van, packing equipment. Halloway stretched muscles cramped from long standing. Duan made notes on her phone. The team dispersed with professional efficiency, the surveillance operation concluded.

"Go home, Miss Blackwell." Frost spoke quietly. "Miss Vance will be there soon. Safe. Happy. Unaware that we were monitoring her date."

"He's using her."

"I know."

"The Council won't authorise action."

"No."

"What do we do?"

Frost's gaze moved to the window, the streetlamp above us flickered, casting his face in alternating shadow and light.

"We gather evidence," he said finally. "Build an ironclad case. Move carefully within the constraints the law provides."

"And if that takes too long? If he moves on Clara before we're ready?"

"Then we'll cross that bridge when we reach it." He met my eyes, and I saw something there that wasn't quite professional—concern, perhaps, or the beginning of something more complicated. "But panicking now serves no purpose except to give Vane exactly what he wants. Your attention divided. Your focus compromised. Your judgment clouded by fear."

The assessment was accurate. It was also useless.

Clara was home when I arrived, still wearing the cream dress with her shoes kicked off, making tea in the kitchen. She hummed that same hopeful melody, her movements light with the bright energy of someone who had spent an evening feeling wanted.

"Imogen!" She looked up as I entered, her expression wary but not hostile. "You're back late."

"Work." I hung my coat, kept my voice neutral. "How was your evening?"

She studied my face, searching for judgment, for the confrontation we'd left unfinished. When she found only careful blankness, some of the tension left her shoulders.

"It was wonderful." The words came out careful, testing. "He was everything I thought. Charming. Interested in my opinions. Asked about my work, my life before..." She gestured vaguely, encompassing all the damage her previous marriage had left. "He made me feel normal."

I sat at the kitchen table. Clara remained standing by the stove, teacup cradled in both hands.

"I'm glad you had a good time."

She blinked. "You're not going to argue?"

"No."

"Or tell me I'm making a mistake?"

"No."

Clara studied my face, searching for the trap.

"What changed?" she asked finally. "An hour ago you were forbidding me from seeing him."

"I was overwrought." I met her eyes, keeping my expression steady. "It has been a very long day. You were right that I sometimes fail to distinguish between professional caution and personal interference."

Truth, delivered with precision. The best lies always were.

The tension in Clara's shoulders eased further. She sat across from me, setting her teacup down.

"He wants to see me again," she said. "Saturday. There's a gallery opening in Chelsea."

"That sounds nice."

"Imogen." She leaned forward slightly. "I know you're trying to protect me. I know you mean well. But I need to live my life. Even if that means making mistakes."

"I understand."

She smiled—small, tentative, genuine. "Thank you."

Then she started talking about the date. The restaurant, the conversation, how Vane had listened when she spoke. How he'd asked intelligent questions. How he'd made her laugh.

I listened. Nodded at appropriate moments. Asked questions that suggested interest rather than interrogation.

And beneath my careful neutrality, I calculated.

Vane had played his opening move. Demonstrated access to Clara. Shown that he could make her happy, could give her the validation she desperately craved. The High Council wouldn't authorise intervention based on suspicion. The M.O.P. couldn't act without probable cause. Clara wouldn't listen to warnings because they sounded like control.

Working within the system wouldn't protect her.

I had spent fifteen years believing in procedure. In proper channels. In the slow, grinding machinery of legal justice. Grimsby had believed in those things too, and they had killed him for it.

Clara deserved better than I could give her through legitimate means.

Which meant finding illegitimate ones.

"I should sleep," Clara said eventually, stifling a yawn. "Long day tomorrow. The bakery has a corporate order."

"Of course." I stood when she did, accepted her brief hug. "Sleep well."

She paused at the kitchen doorway. "Imogen? Thank you. For understanding."

"Always."

She disappeared down the hallway. Her bedroom door closed with a soft click.

I sat alone at the kitchen table, surrounded by the evidence of Clara's happiness—her teacup still warm, her perfume lingering in the air—and began planning how to destroy the man who had given it to her.

Pip emerged from his filing cabinet, climbing onto the table with unusual quietness.

"You did not tell her about the surveillance."

"No."

"You allowed her to believe you accepted her choice."

"Yes."

"You are planning something inadvisable."

I looked at him—fourteen inches of brownie pragmatism wrapped in a waistcoat, amber eyes reflecting the kitchen light with ancient knowing.

"I'm planning something necessary."

"Those are often the same thing." He settled into a seated position, small hands folded. "What do you require?"

"Intelligence. Vane's movements, his schedule, his associates. Everything the M.O.P. can't access because the Council won't authorise surveillance." I pulled a fresh sheet of paper toward me. "You know the brownie networks. Servants in pureblood households who see everything their employers try to hide."

Pip's ears flattened, his whole body rigid. "That violates every neutrality protection I've maintained for three years. The Fae Courts tolerate my independence because I don't organise other brownies or interfere with household service contracts."

"I know what I'm asking."

"Do you?" His ears flattened against his skull. "You are asking me to choose between my professional standing and your personal cause. You are asking me to risk everything I have built because you cannot accept that Miss Vance has the right to make her own mistakes."

"I'm asking you to help me save her life."

The silence stretched. The radiator clanked. Outside, a car passed, its headlights briefly illuminating the kitchen before darkness returned.

"Twenty-four hours," Pip said finally. "I will make inquiries. But if this destroys my network, Miss

Blackwell, you will owe me a debt that contracts cannot measure."

"I understand."

He hopped down from the table and disappeared into his filing cabinet without another word.

I sat alone in the quiet kitchen, pen in hand, and began drafting protection contracts for brownies I'd never met—legal coverage in exchange for intelligence about a man who'd been murdering people for fifteen years.

Outside the window, London continued its double existence. Mundane and magical. Overlapping and hidden.

The law wasn't designed for this. Not for predators who understood its architecture better than the people it claimed to protect. Grimsby had known that, and it had killed him. I knew it now, and it made me faster, colder, more precise.

Chapter 11: The Gathering Storm

The brownie network operated in shadows that aristocratic London pretended not to see.

Pip returned at dawn, climbing through the window I'd left unlatched, his small frame silhouetted against grey morning light. He looked exhausted—ears drooping, waistcoat rumpled, amber eyes dimmed with the weariness of someone who had spent the night calling in favours they couldn't afford to owe.

I was still at the kitchen table, surrounded by the protection contracts I'd spent the night drafting. My hand had cramped around the Null-Ink pen hours ago. I'd kept writing anyway.

"Report." My voice came out rough, abraded by too much tea and too little sleep.

Pip climbed onto the table, stepping carefully around the scattered papers. "The network confirms Julian Vane has reserved a private announcement slot at the Obsidian Hall gala. Tomorrow night. Eleven forty-five, just before midnight."

The words landed like stones in still water.

"What kind of announcement?"

"The household staff couldn't access specifics, but—" Pip hesitated, which was unlike him. "He's ordered flowers. White roses and orange blossoms. Traditional engagement arrangements."

The kitchen felt suddenly airless. White roses for purity. Orange blossoms for fertility and marriage. The symbolic language of aristocratic courtship, centuries old and impossible to misinterpret.

"He's going to propose to Clara."

"Publicly. Before three hundred witnesses. In a venue where refusing him would trigger social catastrophe." Pip's ears flattened against his skull. "The Hall's neutrality laws make social contracts binding when witnessed by enough people. If Clara accepts—or even hesitates long enough to seem like she's considering—the magical weight of three hundred aristocratic expectations will begin forming the engagement bond before she can think clearly."

I stood, needing movement, needing to do something with the fear crystallizing in my chest. The window showed London waking up—delivery trucks, early commuters, the ordinary machinery of a city that had no idea what was being planned in its magical shadows.

"She'll accept," I said. "She'll think it's romantic. The culmination of everything she's wanted—someone who sees her as whole, who values her despite her damaged magic, who offers her entry into a world that's always rejected her."

"Yes."

"And once she accepts, the binding mechanics begin. Even if she changes her mind later, breaking an engagement witnessed at the Obsidian Hall would trigger the Name-Curse. Social isolation. Professional destruction. She'd be marked as someone who led a prominent reformer on, who humiliated him publicly, who can't be trusted."

"Which is exactly when Vane would offer comfort. Understanding. A quick, private ceremony to spare her further public scrutiny." Pip's voice held none of its usual mockery. "The same pattern he's used before. Isolate the target, create dependency, then lock the contract before they can recognise the trap."

I pressed my forehead against the cold glass. Clara was asleep down the hallway, dreaming of whatever dreams people had when they thought love was possible. She had no idea that the man who made her feel seen was calculating her destruction with the precision of a contract clause.

"How do we stop it?"

"That's what the network is still working on." Pip pulled a folded paper from his waistcoat—a hand-drawn map showing the Obsidian Hall's layout. "The venue manifests only during events. No permanent physical location. But there are patterns to how it configures itself, exits that appear in predictable places, ward structures that can be anticipated."

"There are also doors that open elsewhere," Pip added, ears flat. "The Hall sits near a Border Realm threshold—the grey spaces between London's mundane geography and the Void. Smugglers use them. So do people who want to move things—or people—without the M.O.P. noticing. If Vane has access to a Border Realm portal inside the Hall, extraction becomes significantly more complicated."

"We need more than exits. We need evidence compelling enough to break through Clara's emotional investment. Proof so undeniable that even someone desperate to believe in romance can't ignore it."

"Miller is working on the financial records. Green is monitoring communications. Halloway and Duan are gathering tactical intelligence on the Hall's security protocols." Pip met my eyes. "Everyone is working, Miss Blackwell. But we have less than forty hours, and Vane has been doing this for fifteen years."

The fear in my chest hardened into something colder. More useful.

"Then we work faster."

My office had never held this many people.

Miller arrived first with the complete financial analysis—every connection mapped, every death dated, the full architecture of Vane's scheme laid bare in numbers and names. Green joined by phone, monitoring Vane's communications in real time. Halloway and Duan arrived together in civilian clothes—the deliberate statement of off-duty officers pursuing personal interests on their own time.

We already knew what Vane was. The question now was how to stop him before the Obsidian Hall gala gave him his next victim.

"The Hall's neutrality laws prevent violence," Duan said, leaning against the filing cabinet. "But they don't prevent leaving. If we can convince Miss Vance to walk out voluntarily before any announcements are made, the Hall's protections actually work in our favour. Vane can't stop her without breaking neutrality himself."

"Assuming she agrees to leave." Halloway's voice rumbled low. "If she's been convinced this is a romantic gesture, she won't want our interference."

Pip climbed onto my shoulder, surveying the assembled conspiracy. "The household network provided Vane's schedule for the gala. He arrives at nine, mingles until eleven, then guides Clara to a specific location near the eastern alcove where announcements are traditionally made. The proposal is planned for eleven forty-five, with the official announcement at midnight."

"That gives us a window." I moved to the wall where I'd pinned connections and timelines. "Between his arrival and eleven, we need to either extract Clara or present evidence so damning she questions everything."

"What kind of evidence?" Miller asked.

"The murder pattern. The financial fraud. The testimony of surviving victims." I traced the web of connections with one finger. "Clara knows I believe Vane is dangerous, but she thinks I'm projecting personal fears. She needs to hear it from someone else. Someone she has no reason to distrust."

"The widow testimonies," Duan said slowly. "The women whose husbands Vane drained. Some of them are still alive, still carrying the contracts that destroyed their families. If one of them was willing to speak to Miss Vance directly—"

"Would they?" I turned to face her. "Would any of them be willing to confront Vane's latest target?"

Duan's expression was complicated—professional caution warring with something more personal. "Mrs. Pemberton might. Her husband was the fourth victim. She's been asking questions, pushing for investigation, refusing to accept the official explanation of natural causes. If I explained what was at stake..."

"Do it." The decision came without hesitation. "Find her. Explain the situation. Ask if she's willing to meet Clara before the gala."

"And if Clara won't listen?" Miller closed his folder with a snap. "If she's so invested in believing Vane is genuine that she dismisses the testimony as jealousy or manipulation?"

"Then we try something else. And something else after that." I met his eyes. "We have forty hours. I'm not spending any of them assuming failure."

The office fell quiet. Outside, London continued its morning—traffic sounds, distant conversations, the ordinary noise of a city that didn't know three hundred aristocrats were preparing to witness a murder disguised as romance.

"Assignments," I said, pulling a fresh sheet of paper toward me. "Pip, continue coordinating with the brownie network. I need Vane's exact movements, his associates at the gala, any last-minute changes to his plans."

"Done."

"Miller, complete the financial analysis. I want a timeline showing every death connected to Vane's consulting business, with dates and monetary flows. Make it clear enough that someone without forensic training can understand the pattern."

"I'll have it by tonight."

"Green, monitor all communications. If Vane contacts Clara or anyone connected to the gala, I need to know immediately."

"Already set up." The keyboard sounds continued. "You'll receive encrypted alerts."

"Halloway, Duan. Tactical preparation. If we need to extract Clara quickly, what's the plan? What resources do we need? What are the legal and magical constraints on acting inside the Obsidian Hall?"

Halloway and Duan exchanged a look—wordless communication between partners who'd worked together long enough to share shorthand.

"We'll map every exit," Halloway said. "Interview people who've worked events there. Have contingency plans for multiple scenarios."

"And Inspector Frost?" Miller asked. "Where does he fit in this operation?"

The question hung in the air. I'd been avoiding thinking about Frost—about his official position, his institutional obligations, the line between supporting an investigation and enabling vigilantism.

"Frost gave orders to focus on other cases," Duan said carefully. "He didn't specifically forbid anyone from pursuing personal interests on their own time."

"That's not an answer."

"It's the only answer available." I kept my voice steady. "Frost is a High Council Inspector with obligations to institutional authority. What we're planning—surveillance, intervention, possibly interference with a social ceremony on neutral ground—falls outside official sanction. I won't ask him to risk his career for something he can't officially support."

"And if he chooses to risk it anyway?"

"Then that's his choice to make."

The words felt inadequate. Everything about this felt inadequate—a handful of people with conflicting loyalties, planning to stop a predator who had operated freely for fifteen years. The odds were terrible.

But Clara was somewhere in this city, humming hopeful melodies, dreaming of a romance that would destroy her.

The odds were what they were. We'd work with them anyway.

A package arrived that afternoon, delivered by a courier who didn't wait for signature.

The box bore the Stern family crest embossed on the lid—raised silver against black card stock, the kind of expense that signalled old money and older magic. Pip circled it twice, ears flat with suspicion.

"That's aristocratic stationery. Why is Lady Augusta sending you packages?"

"Excellent question."

The tissue paper rustled as I lifted the lid. Deep burgundy silk lay inside, carefully folded, with a sealed envelope resting on top bearing my name in Augusta's unmistakable copperplate.

The note was written on heavy cardstock, criticism codified in elegant script:

Miss Blackwell,

If you insist on attending events beyond your station, the least you can do is avoid embarrassing my nephew through your ignorance. The enclosed gar-

ment is appropriate for the Obsidian Hall. Wear sensible shoes beneath it. Your spectacles are acceptable; remove them and you'll be blind within minutes once Thread Sight activates.

When greeting Council members, use full titles. Address Duke of Ash as "Your Grace." Do not attempt conversation with Baroness Fell unless she initiates. Stand to Lord Frost's left when you must be seen together; standing to his right implies romantic rather than professional association.

The Hall manifests at the Mayfair address enclosed. Arrive no earlier than nine o'clock. Leave before the dancing begins if you value your reputation.

I expect you will ignore that final instruction.

—Lady Augusta Stern

I turned the note over, searching for additional meaning in the blank reverse, and found none.

"She sent you a gown and etiquette coaching." Pip climbed onto the desk to examine the silk. "That's surprisingly helpful. Also definitely a trap."

"Probably." The fabric slid through my fingers—quality evident in the weight and drape, a high neckline and long sleeves designed to allow movement while mimicking elegance. "She claims this is to prevent me embarrassing Frost."

"Do you believe that?"

"No." Augusta's warning at the Tribunal had been genuine, her censure of Frost's association with me equally real. Now this—assistance that contradicted her stated position. "But I'll take the help regardless of motive."

The gown was beautiful, in the way weapons could be beautiful. Armour disguised as elegance. Protection wrapped in silk.

I folded it carefully and set it aside. Tomorrow night, I would wear Augusta's gift into Augusta's world and attempt to destroy a man that world had sheltered for fifteen years.

The irony was not lost on me.

Clara found me that evening, packing a small bag with supplies I couldn't explain—warding stones, salt packets, the Null-Ink pen that had once belonged to Grimsby.

"Working late again?" She leaned against my bedroom doorway, arms crossed, expression caught between affection and exasperation. "You've barely eaten today. Pip says you haven't slept since yesterday."

"I have a complicated case."

"You always have a complicated case." She pushed off the doorframe and came to sit on the edge of my bed. "Imogen. Talk to me. What's going on?"

I looked at her—strawberry blonde hair loose around her shoulders, comfortable cardigan wrapped against the flat's perpetual chill, face open with the open trust of someone who believed I would never lie to her.

"I have to attend an event tomorrow night," I said carefully. "Professional obligation. It may run late."

"The contract review you mentioned? The one with the fancy dress?"

"Yes."

"Is it dangerous?"

The question deserved honesty. I gave her something adjacent to it instead.

"The people involved are powerful. The stakes are significant. I need to be prepared for multiple outcomes."

Clara studied my face with the sharp focus of someone who had survived trauma by learning to read unspoken threats. "You're not telling me something."

"I'm telling you what I can."

"That's not the same thing."

"No. It's not."

Between us hung everything I couldn't say—that the man she loved was a murderer, that tomorrow night he planned to trap her in a contract that would destroy her, that I was assembling a team of rule-breakers to stop him through methods the law couldn't sanction.

"Imogen." Clara's voice softened. "Whatever this is, whatever you're not telling me—please be careful. I can't lose you."

The words hit somewhere beneath my professional armour. I reached out and took her hand, feeling the familiar calluses from her baking work, the faint tremor that never quite went away.

"You won't lose me."

"Promise?"

I thought of the Obsidian Hall, its neutrality laws, the predator waiting to claim her before three hundred witnesses. I thought of the odds we were facing and the inadequacy of our preparations and the terrible truth that promises meant nothing without the power to enforce them.

"I promise to come home," I said. "Whatever happens."

She squeezed my hand once, then released it. "Julian's taking me to the gala tomorrow night. The Obsidian Hall. He says it's an important social event, that he wants to introduce me to people who matter."

The words landed like blows.

"I know."

"You know?" Clara's eyebrows rose. "How do you know?"

"I know because I'll be there too." I held her gaze, letting her see the truth beneath my careful neutrality. "Different reasons. Same venue. We may cross paths."

"Imogen—"

"If we do, please trust me. Whatever happens, whatever it looks like, please trust that I'm trying to help."

Clara's expression shifted through confusion, suspicion, and finally something that looked almost like fear. "You're scaring me."

"I know. I'm sorry." I turned back to my packing, unable to face the questions in her eyes. "I can't explain more than that. Not yet. But by tomorrow night, you'll understand everything."

She was quiet for a long moment. I heard her breathing, heard the creak of the bed as she shifted her weight, heard the question she didn't ask hanging in the air between us.

"All right," she said finally. "I trust you. I don't understand, but I trust you."

"Thank you."

She rose and moved toward the door. Paused at the threshold.

"Imogen? Whatever complicated case this is, whatever powerful people and significant stakes—don't forget that you matter too. Not just as a Scribe, not just as someone who protects others. You matter."

Then she was gone, footsteps retreating down the hallway toward her room.

I sat on the edge of my bed, surrounded by the tools of tomorrow's operation, and tried to believe that mattering would be enough.

The team reconvened at midnight.

My office was too small for comfortable gathering, but comfort wasn't the priority. Miller spread his completed financial analysis across every available surface. Duan reported that Mrs. Pemberton had agreed to meet Clara at the gala—a brief conversation in a private alcove, widow to potential victim, truth delivered without institutional filter.

Halloway produced hand-drawn schematics of the Obsidian Hall's typical configuration. "Three main exits. Two emergency portals that activate if violence threatens. The eastern alcove where announcements are made has limited egress—deliberate design to trap the attention of the crowd."

"If we need to extract Clara during the announcement, we'll have approximately ninety seconds before the social binding begins to crystallize," Duan added. "After that, breaking her away becomes exponentially more difficult."

Green's voice crackled through the phone. "Communications monitoring shows Vane made three calls this afternoon. One to a jeweler—presumably for the engagement ring. One to the Hall's coordinator confirming his announcement slot. And one to a number I haven't traced yet, seventeen minutes, content unknown."

"The unknown call concerns me," Pip said from his position on the filing cabinet. "Seventeen minutes suggests substantive discussion, not casual contact."

"Can you trace it?"

"Working on it. The number routes through several exchanges designed to obscure origin. Someone wants that call invisible."

I looked at the assembled pieces—financial evidence, tactical plans, widow testimony, communication surveillance. More resources than I'd ever had for any case. Still not enough to guarantee success.

"Tomorrow night," I said. "We have one chance. Either we convince Clara to see Vane clearly, or we watch him lock her into a contract that will kill her slowly."

"What about official intervention?" Miller asked. "If Frost attended in his official capacity—"

"The Hall's neutrality laws prevent law enforcement action without proof of immediate physical threat. Vane is too smart to provide that proof until he's ready." I shook my head. "We can't rely on institutional authority. The institution has spent fifteen years protecting him."

"Then we're operating completely outside sanctioned channels."

"Yes."

The word hung in the air. Everyone in this room understood what it meant—careers risked, rules broken, the possibility of consequences none of us could predict.

"I can't ask any of you to do this," I continued. "What we're planning falls outside every protocol that's supposed to protect us. If it goes wrong—"

"Miss Blackwell." Halloway's voice cut through my disclaimer. "We're here. Stop asking permission we've already given."

Duan nodded. Miller closed his folder with quiet finality. Green's keyboard sounds ceased, replaced by purposeful silence.

Pip climbed onto my shoulder, his small weight familiar and grounding.

"Then we have our plan," I said. "Tomorrow night, the Obsidian Hall. We stop Julian Vane, or we fail trying."

"We won't fail." Duan's voice carried the certainty of someone who had talked to the dead and carried their grievances. "Those victims deserve better than another name on the list."

"Clara deserves better," Miller added.

"Then let's make sure she gets it."

The meeting dispersed. Miller gathered his documents. Halloway and Duan left together, already discussing tactical details in low voices. Green disconnected with a promise to maintain monitoring through the night.

I sat alone in my office, surrounded by the evidence of conspiracy and the weight of tomorrow's stakes.

The burgundy gown hung on the back of my door, Augusta's gift waiting to be worn into battle. The Null-Ink pen sat in my pocket, Grimsby's legacy ready to be used against the same system that had killed him.

Somewhere in London, Julian Vane was preparing flowers and rings and the charming words he would use to bind Clara into destruction.

Somewhere closer, Clara was dreaming of romance and acceptance and a future that would never exist.

And somewhere in between, I was planning to burn it all down.

Tomorrow night.

One chance.

I reached for the pen and began drafting the contracts I hoped I wouldn't need—dissolution clauses, emergency nullification terms, the legal framework for destroying a binding before it could fully form.

The work carried me through the dark hours. Outside, London slept. Inside, I prepared for war.

Chapter 12: The Obsidian Hall

The Mayfair address led to an unmarked townhouse door identical to fifty others on the street.

I stood on the pavement in Augusta's burgundy gown, checking the note against the building number, confirming I had the correct location. The boned bodice held my shoulders back, kid gloves sealed my hands in place, and my hair was pinned high enough to expose my throat to the night like a wager. The October evening had turned cold, and my breath misted in the air. Somewhere behind these cream facades and black iron railings, three hundred aristocrats were gathering to witness a murder disguised as romance.

The brass door handle warmed under my palm—magic, obvious and deliberate, an invitation coded into metal that recognised I had permission to enter.

The door swung inward.

No foyer. No entrance hall. Just a corridor of black marble extending impossibly beyond the townhouse's physical footprint, perspective warping as it stretched toward distant light.

I stepped across the threshold of the Obsidian Hall and immediately regretted the clarity of my vision.

The ballroom stretched impossible distances in every direction. Black marble floors reflected like dark water, creating the disorienting impression of walking on liquid shadow—every guest appeared twice, surface and reflection moving in perfect synchronization. The ceiling disappeared into darkness overhead, height unknowable, making the space feel simultaneously vast and pressing. Floating chandeliers provided illumination without casting shadows, everything lit evenly, depth perception failing.

My Thread Sight didn't ask permission. It snapped into focus, overlaying the ballroom with the brutal geometry of influence—gold patronage bonds, crimson blood-debts, silver marriage contracts, and black coercion knots creating a three-dimensional web so dense it made my eyes water. Hundreds of connections, thousands, all visible simultaneously, all demanding attention and analysis.

I pressed my spectacles higher on my nose. The gesture provided no actual help but offered familiar comfort while my mind tried to process impossible information.

"Miss Imogen Blackwell." A servant materialized at my elbow—minor fae in black livery, movements too precise, skin too smooth. "Scribe."

His voice carried unnaturally through the cavernous space, announcing my arrival to hundreds of guests who turned as one to assess this newcomer.

The silence that followed had weight to it. Three hundred pairs of eyes calculating my worth, my connections, my leverage, and finding the sum inadequate. The pressure made breathing require conscious effort.

The servant gestured toward a shallow staircase I hadn't noticed, marble steps descending into the main floor. My legs managed three steps down before muscle memory took over, years of courtroom composure translating into automatic grace.

Frost waited at the base of the stairs.

He wore a formal black tailcoat over a white waistcoat, white gloves covering hands I knew bore calluses from ward-work. His hair was controlled with military precision, silver at the temples catching the shadowless light. The pocket watch chain traced a silver line across his chest.

He extended his arm without smiling. "Miss Blackwell."

I placed my hand lightly on his sleeve, and the contact provided an anchor point—solid reality in the overwhelming space.

He guided me away from the entrance, head bent slightly as if making polite conversation. "Duke of Ash is positioned in the eastern alcove. Baroness Fell has claimed the refreshment area. Vane arrived thirty minutes ago alone. Miss Vance is expected within the hour."

"Exits?"

"Three doorways along the southern wall. Only the leftmost leads back to London." His hand covered mine briefly, keeping me close. "The others access service areas or... elsewhere."

The Border Realm. He didn't say it, but the implication settled cold in my stomach.

We walked a slow circuit of the room's perimeter. Frost acknowledged acquaintances with slight nods, never stopping, maintaining professional distance through body language that broadcast *consultant, not companion.*

"Vane requested the midnight announcement slot three weeks ago," Frost continued. "The duke confirmed it yesterday. It's registered, formal, irreversible once declared under the Hall's neutral-ground magic."

I saw Vane before he saw me.

He stood near the refreshment table with a cluster of minor nobility, glass in hand, laughing at something Lord Pemberton's son had said. The laughter was perfectly calibrated—warm enough to suggest genuine amusement, modest enough to avoid upstaging his companions. He touched the young lord's shoulder with casual affection, the gesture of an older brother rather than a social climber.

Through Thread Sight, I watched him work. Every word generated a thin golden thread of social obligation—not predatory, not yet, just the natural accumulation of goodwill that came from making people feel important. He remembered names, asked after children and investments with specific detail that implied genuine interest. When a dowager countess mentioned her late husband's failing health in the months before his death, Vane's expression shifted to something that looked remarkably like compassion.

"He's very good," I murmured to no one. Frost had drifted to a neighbouring group, maintaining sight lines while pretending to examine a painting. His voice came low from behind a champagne flute.

"The best predators always are." Vane turned, sensing observation with an instinct honed by fifteen years of operating in rooms exactly like this. His gaze found mine across twenty feet of marble floor. He smiled—the same warm, disarming expression he gave everyone—and raised his glass in a small salute.

I didn't return it. His smile widened fractionally, as if my hostility amused him, and he returned his attention to Lord Pemberton's son without missing a conversational beat.

"How long until midnight?" He checked the pocket watch, thumb pressing the release with the precision of long habit. "Two hours and forty-three minutes." Not enough time. Never enough time.

"Mrs. Pemberton?" I kept my voice low.

"Arrived twenty minutes ago. Duan is coordinating. If we can get Clara alone for even five minut es..."

The servant's voice rang out from the staircase. "Mr. Julian Vane and Miss Clara Vance."

My hand tightened on Frost's arm hard enough that he paused mid-step.

Vane ascended the stairs first, at ease in formal evening wear—charcoal tailcoat, perfectly tied cravat, the easy confidence of a man who belonged in spaces like this. He turned at the top, offering his hand down to Clara with theatrical gallantry.

She wore cream silk that made her strawberry blonde hair glow in the shadowless light, arranged in an elaborate updo that required professional help. Gold jewellery I'd never seen before glittered at her throat and ears—delicate pieces, expensive, borrowed or purchased specifically for tonight.

She smiled descending the stairs, brilliant and nervous and happy.

Vane kept her hand as they reached the floor, tucking it into his elbow with the grip of ownership. He moved immediately toward a cluster of pureblood families near the eastern alcove, already beginning introductions before Clara had time to orient herself.

Through Thread Sight, I watched golden threads pulse between them—social magic responding to their public appearance, witnesses' attention strengthening the connection with each moment they stood together. But beneath the gold, darker threads coiled. Black binding knots that had nothing to do with affection, woven so subtly into the connection that Clara would never see them without Scribe training.

"I need to reach her," I said.

"Observe first. Document. When the moment comes to intervene, you'll know."

"What if the moment never comes?"

"Then we adapt." He released my arm, stepping away to create professional distance. "Baroness Fell's circle. Northwestern corner. They're discussing something relevant."

He moved toward Duke of Ash's position with military precision, leaving me standing alone near a marble pillar.

The gossip began within minutes of Clara's arrival.

I positioned myself near Baroness Fell's circle, close enough to hear through the warding stone's privacy enhancement. Four women clustered together, all holding crystal champagne glasses, all wearing expressions I recognised from courtrooms—predators identifying prey.

"Such an unusual choice for Mr. Vane." Lady Ashford's fan moved in lazy arcs, her voice pitched for maximum carry while maintaining plausible deniability. "A working-class girl with no family name, attending the Obsidian Hall on a reformer's arm. The precedent alone should concern anyone who values proper procedure."

"What claim could she possibly make on his estate should he die?" Another voice, higher, sharper. "None that would hold up to review."

"Perhaps Mr. Vane intends to make her legitimate." The fan snapped open again. "A marriage would erase her unfortunate origins. His status would become hers—along with all the inheritance rights she currently lacks."

"How romantic. And how convenient for her."

Through Thread Sight, I watched the damage unfold in real-time. Black threads formed in the air around Clara's position, parasitic binding knots fed by each repetition. The Name-Curse mechanics required seven speakers to manifest fully. Baroness Fell's circle provided four. Their husbands, positioned nearby and nodding agreement, made eight.

The curse was already self-sustaining.

Clara had no idea. She stood beside Vane, answering questions from Lady Ashford with careful formality, using language she'd clearly practised. Trying so hard to be worthy of this space, these people, the romance she thought she'd found.

I deactivated the warding stone and moved away from the pillar before the rage building in my chest manifested as something visible.

Sir Reginald intercepted me halfway across the floor.

"Miss Blackwell." He appeared at my elbow with champagne in hand, his elaborate cravat catching the light. "How delightful to see Scribes attending social events. Tell me, are you here professionally, or has our dear Inspector finally developed interests beyond duty?"

He positioned himself to block my path, requiring engagement.

"Professional consultation, Sir Reginald. Nothing more exciting than contract review."

"Mmm." He touched my arm with familiar presumption. "And Mr. Vane's upcoming announcement? Surely you've heard the rumors?"

"I don't follow society gossip."

"No?" His smile suggested disbelief. "How refreshing. Though I confess surprise at your presence. The Obsidian Hall isn't typically known for welcoming working professionals."

Every sentence contained a barb, every pause implied something offensive he was too polite to say directly. The Obsidian Hall was built for people like Sir Reginald—advocates and aristocratic families who argued before the Council in powdered wigs and silk robes. Barristers' territory. I was a solicitor from Clerkenwell with ink-stained fingers and a rented gown, and every person in this room could smell the difference. I extracted myself with murmured excuses and moved toward Clara's position, determined to intercept her despite Vane's defensive placement.

He saw me coming. His smile never wavered, but his hand tightened on Clara's arm, guiding her smoothly into a different conversational group. Bodies filled the space between us—three pureblood couples engaged in animated discussion about ward maintenance and property disputes.

I could push through. Cause a scene. Force the confrontation. And prove every criticism correct. The working-class radical disrupting aristocratic civility. The outsider who didn't belong, couldn't follow proper protocol, brought chaos to ordered society.

Vane would position Clara as the victim of my aggression—the sweet hedgewitch being harassed by her overbearing former employer who couldn't accept that Clara had moved beyond their cramped flat and borrowed respectability.

The gossip would write itself.

I stopped moving and stood watching, helpless.

Duan found me an hour later, her uniform hidden beneath borrowed formal wear that fit poorly.

"Mrs. Pemberton is ready," she said quietly. "Private alcove near the refreshments. If you can guide Miss Vance there..."

"I can't get near her. Vane intercepts every approach."

"Then we need a distraction." Duan's eyes swept the room. "Something that pulls his attention long enough for you to reach her."

"What kind of distraction?"

"Leave that to Halloway. He's positioned near the eastern entrance." She pressed a small object into my palm—another warding stone, this one inscribed with symbols I didn't recognise. "When you reach her, activate this. It creates a privacy bubble. Thirty seconds of complete isolation from outside observation. Use the time well."

She disappeared into the crowd before I could respond.

The clock chimed eleven.

One hour remaining.

I moved toward Clara's position with renewed purpose, tracking her through Thread Sight even when bodies blocked my view. The golden threads between her and Vane pulsed steadily, strengthened by each passing minute, but they weren't yet crystallized into formal binding. There was still time.

A commotion near the eastern entrance drew attention. Halloway's voice, raised in apparent argument with a server over some matter of protocol. Guests turned to observe the disturbance, conversations pausing, champagne glasses lowering.

Vane's head turned toward the noise.

I moved.

Three steps, five, threading between distracted couples. Clara stood alone for a single moment, Vane's attention elsewhere, and I reached her side before he could redirect.

"Clara."

She spun, eyes widening. "Imogen? What are you—how did you—"

"I need you to come with me. Now. Just for a moment."

"I don't understand." She glanced toward Vane, who was already turning back, his expression shifting from curiosity to controlled alarm. "Julian said you might be here, but he didn't say why. He said you've been investigating him, that you have some kind of professional grudge—"

"He's lying." I gripped her arm, urgency overriding caution. "Please, Clara. Five minutes. There's someone who needs to tell you something, and then you can decide for yourself what's true."

"Imogen, you're scaring me."

"Good. You should be scared."

Vane appeared at Clara's other side, his warm smile firmly in place. "Miss Blackwell. What a pleasant surprise. Clara mentioned you might attend tonight."

"Mr. Vane." I didn't release Clara's arm. "I was just asking Clara to accompany me to the refreshment area. Girl talk."

"Of course." His smile didn't waver, but his eyes had gone flat. "Though I'm afraid I must steal her back shortly. We have... plans for later this evening."

"Five minutes."

"Certainly." He released Clara with apparent graciousness, but his hand brushed hers in a gesture that was both tender and possessive. "Don't be long, darling. The evening's just beginning."

I guided Clara through the crowd before he could change his mind, steering her toward the alcove where Mrs. Pemberton waited. The privacy stone sat heavy in my palm, ready for activation.

"Imogen, what is going on?" Clara's voice held an edge of real fear now. "Why are you acting like this? Why are you here?"

"Because I love you," I said. "And because the man you think loves you has killed four people that we know of, and he's planning to kill you too."

She stopped walking. "That's insane."

"I know it sounds insane. That's why I'm not asking you to believe me." I pulled her into the alcove's shadow, activating the privacy stone with a whispered word. The world outside went silent, muffled behind an invisible barrier. "I'm asking you to listen to someone else. Someone who has no reason to lie."

Mrs. Pemberton stepped forward from the alcove's depths.

She was older than I'd expected—mid-fifties, grey threading through dark hair, wearing formal mourning that marked her as a recent widow. Her face bore the deep exhaustion of someone who had spent months fighting a system that didn't want to hear her.

"Miss Vance." Her voice was steady, but her hands trembled slightly. "My name is Eleanor Pemberton. Three months ago, my husband was found dead in our home. The official report said natural causes."

Clara's eyes darted between us. "I don't understand what this has to do with—"

"Julian Vane was my husband's financial advisor." Mrs. Pemberton's voice cracked on the name. "He helped us restructure our contracts, consolidate our debts. He was charming. Attentive. He made my husband feel like he was finally getting control of our family's finances."

"That doesn't mean—"

"Six months after Julian began advising us, my husband started having health problems. Fatigue. Memory loss. Difficulty with magic he'd performed his entire life." Mrs. Pemberton's hands clenched in her skirt. "The healers couldn't find anything wrong. But I watched him fade. Day by day, week by week. Like something was draining him from the inside."

Clara had gone very pale.

"When he died," Mrs. Pemberton continued, "I found contracts in his study. Documents he'd signed without telling me. Clauses that allowed Julian to extract what he called 'consulting fees' from our family's magical reserves. Soul equity, the contracts called it." Her voice dropped to a whisper. "Julian was harvesting my husband's power. Using our contracts to drain him until there was nothing left."

"That's... that's not possible." Clara's voice shook. "Julian helps people. He's a reformer. He advocates for working-class access to—"

"He advocates for access because it gives him new victims." Mrs. Pemberton stepped closer, and I saw tears tracking down her cheeks. "People like us. People without powerful families to protect us. People desperate enough to trust someone who seems to understand."

The privacy bubble flickered. Thirty seconds was nearly gone.

"Clara," I said. "I have financial records showing Julian's pattern. Death after death, all connected to his consulting business. All preceded by the same contract modifications. All leaving him richer and his clients dead."

"I don't believe you." But her voice lacked conviction. Her hand had moved to her chest, pressing against the gold necklace Julian had given her. "He loves me. He said—"

"He said what you needed to hear." Mrs. Pemberton's voice was gentle now, the anger giving way to something like pity. "That's what he does. He finds what you're missing—validation, acceptance, hope—and he offers it freely until you're bound so tightly you can't escape."

The privacy bubble collapsed.

Sound rushed back—music, conversation, the clink of crystal glasses. Clara stood frozen, her face a battlefield of competing emotions. I watched her processing, calculating, trying to reconcile the man who made her feel whole with the predator we were describing.

"I need to think," she said finally. "I need—"

"Clara, darling." Vane's voice came from behind us, warm and concerned. "Is everything all right? You look upset."

He stood at the alcove's entrance, his expression perfectly calibrated to suggest worried affection. But his eyes moved between Mrs. Pemberton and me with cold calculation, assessing how much damage had been done.

"Julian." Clara turned to face him, and I saw her mask slide into place—the practised smile, the controlled posture. "I'm fine. Just overwhelmed. So many people, so much attention."

"Of course, darling. It's a lot to take in." He extended his hand. "Come. Let me introduce you to some friends who are much less intimidating."

Clara hesitated. For one moment—one endless moment—I saw the doubt in her eyes. The questions forming. The possibility of choosing differently.

Then she took his hand.

"It was nice to meet you, Mrs. Pemberton," she said, her voice carefully neutral. "I'm sorry for your loss."

She walked away with Vane, leaving me standing in the alcove with a widow's tears and the bitter taste of failure.

The clock chimed eleven-thirty.

Servants began lighting additional candelabras around the central dais—the raised platform where announcements were traditionally made, three shallow steps leading to a space designed for public declaration.

Vane moved toward it with Clara still on his arm.

She looked confused but pleased, thinking this was part of the evening's entertainment. He positioned her at the dais's base, keeping his hand on her lower back in a gesture that was both protective and proprietary.

Other guests gravitated toward the edges of the floor space, forming an audience. Social instinct drawing them to witness whatever was about to happen.

Frost materialized beside me. "Thirty minutes."

"I can't stop it." The words tasted bitter. "Any intervention before he speaks makes us the aggressors. We violate the Hall's neutrality, destroy our credibility, give him exactly the narrative he needs."

"And after?"

"The social contract forms. Clara feels obligated to accept or face the Name-Curse that's been building all evening. Refusing him publicly becomes refusing the entire aristocratic structure that's accepted her tonight. The weight of three hundred witnesses will make her refusal a binding breach."

Frost's hand found mine in the shadow—brief contact, breaking half a dozen etiquette rules. "We'll convince her to leave. Show her everything. Extract her before any binding ceremony can occur."

"If she'll listen."

"She must."

The clock began chiming midnight.

Twelve resonant tones that fell like hammer blows, demanding attention, making conversation cease mid-sentence, forcing every guest to turn toward the central dais.

Vane took Clara's hand, leading her up the three steps to the platform. She followed, surprised and delighted, still unaware of the trap closing around her.

He positioned her beside him, facing the assembled crowd. Three hundred supernatural beings falling silent in unison, their combined attention providing magical weight that made the air itself feel dense with pending obligation.

Golden threads between Vane and Clara blazed brighter, fed by the witnesses' focus.

"Friends." Vane's voice carried without amplification, minor magic ensuring every word reached every ear. "Allies. Members of this august assembly."

His warm smile encompassed the entire room.

"Tonight I stand before you with joy in my heart and hope for our community's future."

He turned to Clara, taking both her hands. She blushed, understanding finally beginning to dawn.

"The old ways taught us that power comes from ancient bloodlines. That worth is measured in magical capacity and family name. That working-class supernatural beings exist to serve, not to partner with their betters."

Murmurs rippled through the audience—approval from some, skepticism from others.

"But I believe we can be better. That love transcends class. That choosing a partner for affection rather than strategic alliance represents the highest form of magic."

The golden threads pulsed with each word, social magic responding to rhetorical power.

"Clara Vance." He spoke her name with warmth that sounded absolutely real. "You have shown me that happiness exists beyond duty, that kindness matters more than pedigree, that a life spent in partnership exceeds any amount of inherited power."

Clara's eyes glistened. Her free hand pressed against her chest, over her heart.

"Would you do me the extraordinary honour of becoming my wife?"

The Hall held its breath. Three hundred witnesses suspended in the moment between question and answer, their attention creating binding pressure that made refusal impossible without catastrophic cost.

Clara's mouth opened.

"Yes." Her voice carried across the ballroom, soft and trembling and delighted. "Yes, I'll marry you."

Applause broke out—a polite, thundering wave that drowned the room.

I stood twenty feet away, separated by rows of aristocratic bodies, and watched golden threads shimmer into existence between them. The engagement bond, forming in real-time, powered by three hundred witnesses whose attention provided magical weight to the declaration.

Too late for privacy bubbles. Too late for quiet intervention.

Through Thread Sight, I watched the binding crystallize—gold and black threads weaving together, Clara's remaining magical essence beginning to flow toward Vane through channels she couldn't see. The extraction had already begun, disguised as connection, masked as love.

Vane turned Clara to face him fully. He said something too quiet for me to hear, then gestured toward the northeastern alcove.

"Just for a moment, darling. To celebrate properly before we rejoin the festivities."

A doorway materialized in the alcove—ornate carved wood that hadn't existed minutes earlier, showing grey fog beyond instead of corridor. Border Realm portal. Unregulated. A smuggling route masquerading as architecture.

He was taking her out of London entirely.

Somewhere the M.O.P. had no jurisdiction. Somewhere he could complete whatever ritual required privacy and absolute isolation.

Somewhere he could drain her completely.

I abandoned all pretense and ran.

Sir Reginald intercepted me before I'd cleared ten feet, his grip on my elbow masquerading as solicitude. "Miss Blackwell. You look unwell. Perhaps some air?"

"Let go."

"I really must insist." His fingers tightened. "You're making a scene."

Lord Ashford moved to my left, his bulk creating a wall. Baroness Fell glided forward from the right. Three more couples positioned themselves between me and the portal, their conversation never pausing but their bodies forming an impenetrable barrier.

I wrenched against Sir Reginald's grip. "Clara! Don't go through that door!"

She stopped walking.

Five feet from the threshold, Clara turned her head back toward the ballroom. Searching. Her free hand touched the gold necklace at her throat.

Vane's grip on her other hand tightened. He leaned close, whispering something into her ear while maintaining that warm smile for the watching crowd.

Whatever he said made her relax. She nodded, laughed—nervous and flattered. They resumed walking toward the portal.

"Inspector Frost!" My voice cracked. "Stop him!"

Frost strode from his position near Duke of Ash, his Inspector's badge visible on its silver chain. He positioned himself between Vane's group and the portal, one hand raised in formal arrest gesture.

"Julian Vane. By order of the Metropolitan Occult Police, you are commanded to remain within this jurisdiction for questioning."

Duke of Ash rose from his chair.

The ancient vampire moved with inhuman speed, crossing thirty feet in the span of a breath. His presence forced Frost back one step through sheer proximity to predator.

"Inspector Frost." The duke's voice resonated with centuries of power. "The Obsidian Hall maintains absolute neutrality. No law enforcement action may be taken within these walls without proof of immediate physical threat to assembled guests."

"The evidence exists. Multiple murders. Contract fraud. Predatory binding. Your Grace, this man is dangerous."

"Alleged crimes committed in London are London's problem." Duke of Ash's smile showed teeth. "The Hall's neutrality is absolute. If Mr. Vane has committed crimes beyond these walls, you may arrest him when he departs through mundane London." The pause felt deliberate. "Should he choose to depart that way."

Behind them, Vane guided Clara through the doorway.

She stepped into grey fog and vanished from view.

"No!"

I wrenched against Sir Reginald's grip hard enough that something in my shoulder gave. Pain lanced down my arm but his fingers released.

I ran.

Lord and Lady Ashford stepped through the portal. Three other couples followed in practised sequence.

Vane paused on the threshold.

He turned back to face the ballroom, finding me in the crowd. Our eyes met across forty feet of space. His warm smile became something else entirely—colder, victorious. Acknowledging that I'd lost and he'd won and Clara's destruction was my failure.

Then he stepped through and disappeared.

The portal began closing. The carved doorway shimmered, edges dissolving into mist. grey fog became opaque. The doorway itself started shrinking—eight feet becoming seven, six, five.

I reached the threshold as it collapsed completely.

My fists hit solid marble. I struck the wall repeatedly, searching for any give, any trace of magical signature that would allow reconstruction. Thread Sight showed nothing. The portal had dissolved without leaving anchor points.

Behind me, the ballroom resumed its scandalized whispers.

"...that Scribe woman making a scene..."

"...precisely what one expects from working-class presumption..."

I pressed both palms flat against the marble where Clara had vanished. The stone was cold, ancient, unmoved by my desperation.

"Imogen."

Frost appeared at my shoulder. He held his pocket watch between us, and I saw the silver case was obscured by a layer of white rime rapidly spreading to his glove. The air around him dropped twenty degrees.

He held the watch to my ear.

The mechanism wasn't ticking. It was limping. Skip. Skip. Beat. Silence.

"The wards are failing." His voice remained controlled but urgency edged every word. "Someone is attacking the seal directly."

The timing was too precise to be accidental. The portal. The seal. Two strikes, one clock.

"This was coordinated," I said. "Vane knew exactly when to take Clara through. Someone timed an attack on your family's estate to coincide with the announcement."

Frost nodded once, sharp and controlled. His free hand gripped my shoulder—three seconds of contact that violated every etiquette rule before releasing.

"If the seal fails, thousands die. The Void will consume everything within a mile of Ashwood Manor." He stepped back, putting physical distance between us. "I cannot..."

He stopped. His jaw worked as competing obligations warred visibly across his features.

"Go." I straightened, forcing myself to stop touching the wall. "Now. I'll find her."

"Miss Blackwell..."

"There are other ways into the Border Realm. I have contacts. Resources." I met his eyes directly. "Clara has maybe an hour before he completes whatever ritual he's planning. The Void seal cannot wait even that long."

Frost didn't move for five heartbeats. The rime-covered watch ticked its warning.

"I will return as quickly as possible." Military language, seeking comfort in formality. "Hold the line until then."

He turned and strode toward the main entrance, long coat swirling. The assembled guests parted to create a path, then closed ranks after he passed.

I watched him disappear through the doorway.

Then turned back to face the ballroom alone.

Three hundred aristocrats stared at me. The conversations that had paused during Frost's departure resumed with increased animation, the scandal providing fresh entertainment.

"...that Scribe woman..."

"...attacking the wall like a common criminal..."

"...Miss Vance's unfortunate association with rad icals..."

Each comment fed the Name-Curse spreading through the room. Through Thread Sight, I watched Clara's reputation being destroyed in real-time by aristocratic voices speaking in unison. I smoothed the front of Augusta's silk like it was armour, then stilled my gloved fingers—refusing to give the watching room even one visible crack to widen.

But Clara wasn't here to suffer it.

Clara was somewhere in the Border Realm, in the hands of a man who had murdered four people and planned to make her the fifth.

I pulled my mobile from the gown's hidden pocket and dialed Pip's number with fingers that wanted to shake.

"Miss Blackwell?" His voice was sharp with alertness. "What's happened?"

"She's gone. Vane took her through a portal. Border Realm access, northeastern section of the Hall."

"I'll find crossing points. Give me ten minutes."

"We don't have ten minutes."

"Then I'll find them in five." The line crackled. "Miss Blackwell—if we do this, we're operating completely outside official channels. No M.O.P. backup. No legal authority."

"The system just proved it exists to protect people like Vane." I watched the portal's former location, searching for any trace of magical residue. "Clara doesn't have time for me to worry about proper procedure."

"Then we operate without a license?"

"We use every loophole, every underground network, every contact who owes us favours to get

Clara back." I turned away from the wall, away from the scandalized whispers, away from the beautiful cruelty of the Obsidian Hall. "Then we file an appeal by other means."

I walked toward the exit, burgundy silk swirling against my ankles, ignoring the stares and murmurs that followed me through the crowd.

Clara was somewhere in the grey space between worlds.

And I was going to get her back or die trying.

Chapter 13: The Unauthorised Rescue

The flat had never held this many people.

I'd changed out of Augusta's burgundy gown in three minutes flat, trading silk for familiar wool and Oxford shoes that could handle whatever terrain waited in the Border Realm. The work coat went on last, pockets weighted with every tool I owned—Null-Ink pen against my ribs, warding stones, salt packets, iron nails. The mundane arsenal of working-class protection magic.

Pip had worked miracles in the twenty minutes since my call. He perched on the kitchen table now, a hand-drawn map spread before him showing crossing points between London and the grey spaces beyond.

"The Warrens entrance is closest," he said, tracing a route with one small finger. "Thirty minutes of travel through unstable territory before we reach the chapel coordinates."

"Chapel?"

"Abandoned. Dates to the 1640s, used during the Civil War era for—" He paused, ears flattening.

"Magical purges. Contract severance rituals. The architecture was designed to amplify unbinding magic."

The Severing Shears. An artifact from that period, built to cut what should never be cut. Vane wasn't just using them as a murder weapon. He was returning them to their original purpose in a space designed for exactly this kind of destruction.

"How long does Clara have?"

"The ritual requires preparation. Warding stones, blood circles, the proper astronomical alignment." Pip's voice held none of its usual sarcasm. "Based on the portal's destination coordinates, I estimate sixty to ninety minutes before he can begin the actual severance."

Sixty minutes. Maybe ninety. The numbers felt like a countdown timer strapped to my chest.

A knock at the door—three sharp raps, then two.

Miller entered first, tracking equipment slung over one shoulder, wearing the exhausted expression of a man who had stopped asking questions about why his evening kept getting worse. He surveyed the cramped kitchen with the resignation of someone accustomed to inadequate field conditions.

"Signal's still active," he said, setting his bag on the counter. "Whatever Vane did to mask his location, it doesn't extend to Miss Vance. Her magical signature is readable—faint, but consistent with Border Realm interference."

Green followed close behind, laptop already open, fingers moving across keys before she'd fully crossed the threshold. Her purple hair had escaped its usual tie, strands falling across her face as she worked.

"Portal coordinates confirmed. Cross-referencing with known Border Realm structures now." She didn't look up. "The chapel matches historical records. Pre-Victorian, high ambient magic, multiple severance rituals documented in the archives."

Halloway and Duan arrived together, both in civilian clothes—the deliberate statement of off-duty officers pursuing personal interests on their own time. Halloway's bulk made the kitchen feel like a closet. Duan moved past him with practised efficiency, already assessing exits and sight lines.

"Reporting as requested," Halloway said to the empty air.

"No one requested anything." I kept my voice level. "You're not here officially. None of you are."

"Understood." Duan leaned against the counter, arms crossed. "We're not here. This conversation isn't happening. And if something goes wrong—"

"Nothing goes wrong." The words came out harder than intended. "Clara doesn't have time for something to go wrong."

The kitchen fell silent. Five people and one brownie, crammed into a space designed for tea and toast, preparing to cross into a dimension that operated on different rules than anything we understood.

The door opened without a knock.

Frost stood in the hallway, long coat swirling with the motion of his arrival. His face was carved from ice—pale, rigid, betraying nothing. But his eyes found mine immediately, and something in them cracked.

"The seal holds," he said. "Temporarily. I reinforced the wards, but—"

"You should be at Ashwood Manor."

"I should be many places." He stepped inside, closing the door behind him. "I chose to be here."

The words hung between us. I thought of what that choice meant—his family's sacred duty, the Void seal that had been maintained for generations, the thousands of lives that depended on its integrity. He had left all of it for this. For Clara. For me.

"Frost—"

"The seal will hold for six hours. I spoke with my aunt." His jaw tightened almost imperceptibly. "She was... displeased. But she agreed to monitor the wards personally until I return."

Augusta Stern, covering for her nephew's unauthorised rescue mission. The aristocratic politics of that arrangement made my head hurt to contemplate.

"Six hours," I repeated. "That's our window."

"That's our window."

He moved past me to examine Pip's map, and I watched him transform. The long coat came off first, draped over a chair with uncharacteristic carelessness. Then the waistcoat, unbuttoned and set aside. He rolled his sleeves to the elbow with precise, economical movements, revealing the frost-scarred skin of his forearms.

The scar on his left palm was visible now—the mark of his family's anchoring ritual, the physical price of maintaining the Void seal. He'd carried that burden since he was nineteen years old.

He set his M.O.P. badge on the table beside the map. The silver chain pooled around it like a question mark.

"We're operating without official sanction," he said, addressing the room. "No M.O.P. authority. No Council backing. If we're caught, I cannot protect any of you from the consequences."

"Noted," Halloway rumbled. "What's the tactical approach?"

Frost studied the map. "Entry through the Warrens crossing point Pip identified. Standard formation—Halloway on point, Duan at rear. Miller tracks the signal. Green monitors for ward signatures." His eyes met mine. "Miss Blackwell navigates via Thread

Sight. The Border Realm's magic is unstable, but the threads should remain visible."

"And you?" I asked.

"I clear the path." He flexed his scarred hand once, controlled motion that suggested barely contained power. "Vane will have defensive wards. I can break them faster than anyone else present."

The plan was thin. Desperate. The kind of improvised strategy that looked reasonable on paper and fell apart the moment it contacted reality.

It was also the only plan we had.

"Questions?" Frost looked around the kitchen. No one spoke. "Then we leave in two minutes."

The team moved with sudden purpose. Miller checked his equipment. Green closed the laptop and tucked it under one arm. Halloway and Duan exchanged a look that communicated something in the silent language of partners who had worked together for years.

Pip climbed onto my shoulder, settling into his usual position. His small weight was familiar, grounding.

"Miss Blackwell." His voice was quiet enough that only I could hear. "If this goes badly—"

"It won't."

"If it does." He pressed closer to my neck. "I want you to know that working for you has been the most professionally frustrating experience of my existence. Your filing system is chaos. Your client selection is financially suicidal. And your tendency to pursue justice over payment has cost me countless hours of organizational labor."

I blinked. "Is this a complaint?"

"It's a statement of fact." His ears twitched. "Also, I would not trade it for any position in the fae courts. You are the most stubborn, impractical, unreasonably principled human I have ever served. Clara is lucky to have you."

My throat tightened. "Pip—"

"We should go now. I believe Frost is waiting."

I turned to find Frost at the door, watching me with an expression I couldn't read. The kitchen had emptied around us—Miller, Green, Halloway, and Duan already descending the stairs to the street below.

"Ready?" Frost asked.

"No." I buttoned my coat, checked each pocket by touch one final time. "But Clara can't wait for me to be ready."

We walked out into London's pre-dawn darkness together.

The Warrens crossing point waited in a basement beneath a condemned building in Southwark.

Pip had guided us through streets that grew progressively stranger—normal London giving way to the liminal spaces where magic pooled and reality grew thin. The buildings here looked wrong, proportions slightly off, windows reflecting light that came from nowhere visible.

Duan found the entrance behind a rusted door that shouldn't have opened but did. Stairs descended into darkness that swallowed our torchlight rather than reflecting it.

"Charming," Miller muttered. "Very welcoming."

The basement was empty except for a section of wall that shimmered like heat haze over summer pavement. The air tasted of copper and old stone. My skin prickled with the static charge of barely contained magic.

"The crossing point," Pip said from my shoulder. "It's stable for the next four hours. After that, the alignment shifts and we'd need to find a different exit."

"Then we finish this in under four hours." Frost stepped toward the shimmering wall. "Formation. Halloway, you're through first. Secure the immediate area. Duan follows. Then Miller, Green, Miss Blackwell, and myself."

Halloway drew a breath, rolled his massive shoulders, and walked into the shimmer.

He disappeared.

Not gradually—completely. One moment he was there, the next he simply wasn't. The wall rippled once where he'd passed through, then settled back to its steady shimmer.

Duan went next, moving with military precision. She vanished the same way, swallowed by whatever waited on the other side.

Miller adjusted his tracking equipment and stepped through without comment. Green followed, laptop clutched against her chest like armour.

I approached the shimmer. Up close, it smelled of rain on hot pavement and something else—flowers that had never grown in any garden I'd seen. The magic pressed against my skin, testing, tasting.

"Together?" Frost asked from beside me.

"Together."

We stepped through.

The Border Realm was wrong.

Not dangerous, not yet—just fundamentally, viscerally incorrect. grey fog pressed against exposed skin with faint resistance, seeping into joints and knuckles with a chill that had nothing to do with temperature. The ground beneath my feet felt less like geology than memory, shifting between cobblestone and packed earth and something that might have been water frozen mid-ripple.

I activated Thread Sight without conscious decision. The world stripped to its architecture—or tried to. Here, the threads were distorted, stretched thin, colours bleeding into each other like watercolours left in the rain. Gold and silver and red and black, all tangled together, all pointing in directions that didn't correspond to physical space.

But Clara's thread was there. Faint, strained, leading deeper into the fog.

"This way." My voice came out wrong—too loud, then swallowed instantly by the damp air. "The thread is weak but visible."

Halloway had secured a perimeter of approximately ten feet, which was all the visibility the fog allowed. Duan stood at his shoulder, both of them scanning for threats that might emerge from the grey.

"Move," Frost said. "Standard formation. Stay close."

We moved.

The fog swallowed everything beyond arm's reach. Sound distorted—Duan's footsteps seemed to come from the wrong direction, Frost's breathing echoed before the inhale. Whispers suggested voices that weren't there, forming almost-words in languages I didn't recognise.

"Structure ahead," Miller reported, checking his equipment. "Fifty meters, bearing northeast relative to our entry point. The signal's getting stronger."

Fifty meters might as well have been fifty miles. Each step required negotiation with terrain that refused to stay consistent. I stumbled over cobblestones that became mud, caught myself on Frost's arm when the ground dropped six inches without warning.

"Apologies." I released him immediately.

"Don't be." His hand found my elbow, steadying. "The realm tests everyone. It's designed to disorient."

"It's succeeding."

Pip's claws dug into my shoulder through the coat fabric. "This realm is deeply unpleasant. If we survive, I'm filing a formal complaint with whoever maintains it."

"No one maintains it." Green's voice came from somewhere to my right, her position obscured by grey. "It's accumulated magical residue. Centuries of failed rituals and broken contracts bleeding through from London. The realm doesn't have a purpose—it's just... leftovers."

"Delightful. We're walking through magical garbage."

"Essentially."

The temperature fluctuated without pattern. Pockets of warmth gave way to freezing cold, creating disorienting shifts that made my body forget what comfort felt like. The fog tasted different in each pocket—old metal, damp stone, impossible flowers, rain on hot pavement.

My coat felt weighted with moisture that wasn't quite water. The fabric clung to my arms. The tools in my pockets had grown heavier, iron and salt responding to the ambient wrongness.

"There." Duan's voice cut through the confusion. "I see something."

I followed her gaze—or tried to. The fog parted reluctantly, revealing what might have been a structure ahead. Stone walls. A peaked roof. The suggestion of a doorway.

"The chapel," Pip confirmed. "That's the ritual site."

We approached carefully. The building solidified as we drew closer, becoming more real, more present. Pre-Victorian architecture, all grey stone and narrow windows, looking like it had been waiting here since Cromwell's army marched through England.

Waiting for exactly this moment.

Light glowed from within—not natural light, not electrical. Something colder. Something that made the threads in my vision strain and twist.

"Wards," Frost said quietly. "I can feel them. Three layers, maybe four. Designed to alert, then contain, then kill."

"Can you break them?"

"Yes." He stepped forward, rolling his scarred hand into a fist. "But Vane will know the moment I start. We lose any element of surprise."

"Clara's inside with a murderer and a pair of magical shears designed to sever souls from bodies." I met his eyes through the fog. "I don't think surprise was ever really an option."

Something that might have been a smile flickered across his face. "Fair point."

He raised his scarred hand toward the chapel doorway.

And the wards began to scream.

Chapter 14: The Severing

The wards screamed like dying things.

Golden light cracked across the chapel's facade, networks of magical barriers becoming briefly visible as Frost's power shattered them layer by layer. The sound was enormous—glass breaking underwater, metal tearing, something ancient and brittle finally giving way.

Inside the chapel, Vane spun toward the noise.

Through the gaps in the ruined walls, I saw everything with terrible clarity. Clara sat on an elevated altar platform, twelve warding stones forming a perfect circle around her position. Her pastel gown from the Obsidian Hall was dirty at the hem, strawberry blonde curls disheveled. She pressed both palms against an invisible barrier, fingers splayed wide and whitening at the tips.

She knew now. The colour had drained from her face, comprehension arriving too late.

Vane recovered quickly. He moved toward the chapel entrance, the Severing Shears held in his right hand like a weapon rather than an artifact.

The charming warmth from the gala had vanished entirely, replaced by cold calculation.

"Miss Blackwell." His voice carried with unnatural clarity through the fog. "I should have known you'd find a way. You and your working-class tenacity."

"Let her go, Vane."

"Or what? You'll file an appeal?" He smiled, but there was nothing warm in it now. "The Council already denied your warrant. The M.O.P. has no jurisdiction in the Border Realm. And this chapel exists outside every legal framework you've ever used to pretend you had power."

Frost stepped forward, ice already forming along his forearms. "You're under arrest for the murders of Elias Thorne, Marcus Bellingham, Edmund Cartwright, and Lord Pemberton. Additional charges pending for conspiracy, contract fraud, and—"

"Arrest." Vane laughed—a sharp, ugly sound. "Inspector, look around you. We're standing in a dimension that doesn't acknowledge your authority. Your badges mean nothing here. Your procedures mean nothing. The only law that matters is power, and I have been accumulating power for fifteen years while you shuffled paperwork."

He raised his free hand, palm outward.

"Halloway," Frost said quietly. "Now."

Halloway stepped forward, crouched, and slammed both palms into the ground.

The earth rippled outward like water disturbed by a stone—a visible wave traveling toward the chapel. When it hit Vane's defensive wards, the remaining barriers shattered in cascading failure, golden fragments dissolving into sparks that hung in the fog before fading.

Vane staggered but didn't fall. He spoke a word of power, and six translucent shapes materialized from the grey mist—ghostly servants reduced to automatons, moving with clockwork precision to intercept our approach.

"Deal with them," Frost ordered.

Halloway and Miller moved to engage, positioning themselves between the ghosts and the rest of us. Duan flanked left, her movements precise and economical. Green stayed back, laptop balanced on one forearm, attempting to disrupt the servants' programming through technical means.

The fighting drew the ghosts away from the chapel entrance.

Opening.

I ran.

Coat flaring behind me, I sprinted across broken ground toward the Gothic entrance. Vane saw me coming. His free hand extended, fingers splayed, and blue-white fire erupted from his palm—defensive magic that should have incinerated anyone in its path.

I ran straight through it.

The flames parted around my Null signature, unable to perceive me, unable to touch me. The magical heat washed around my body like water around a stone. My coat fabric smoked where the fire tried to grab hold and failed, but my skin remained untouched.

Vane's expression shifted. Confusion replacing confidence. He'd forgotten—or never understood—what it meant to face someone who existed outside magical frameworks entirely.

Behind me, Frost extended both arms forward, palms facing the altar. Words in the old language fell from his lips, syllables older than modern English.

Ice crystallized from nothing. A wall rising between Vane's position and Clara's—transparent blue ice growing from ground level to ten feet high in a matter of heartbeats. Blocking movement. Distorting vision. Buying time.

Vane spun toward the barrier, momentarily distracted.

I hit him with the full force of my momentum.

My hands locked around the Severing Shears' iron handles, fingers finding grip despite the artifact's searing heat. Vane snarled—a sound entirely stripped of his gala-night charm—and twisted the weapon violently. He was stronger, leverage and height on his side, but I held on with the desperate tenacity of someone who had stopped believing in procedure and started believing in results.

We spun in a half-circle, locked together, neither gaining advantage.

The Shears flared white-hot, recognizing the conflict of intent. The magic slid off my skin like rain off oil. I wasn't fighting him with power. I was fighting him with physics, with stubbornness, with the knowledge that Clara was twenty feet away and running out of time.

"You can't win." Vane's voice was strained, muscles trembling with effort. "You're nothing. A Null. A void where magic should be. You don't even register as a person to half the artifacts in this realm."

"Exactly."

I shifted my weight, dropping my center of gravity, using his strength against him. He overbalanced, recovered, changed tactics. Pushed forward instead of pulling, driving the Shears' blades toward my chest in a stabbing motion.

I stumbled backward, maintaining my grip but losing balance. The Shears' points touched my coat, pressing against my sternum.

Vane spoke another power word.

The blades flared with white light, hot enough that smoke rose from my coat fabric. The artifact was trying to sever something—searching for the threads that bound my life to my body, the magical connections that made a person a person.

Nothing happened.

The Severing Shears could cut any binding. But they couldn't perceive a Null's life threads. I existed outside magical frameworks. The weapon that could sever any contract couldn't affect someone who had never been bound.

Vane's eyes widened with understanding that came too late.

I released the Shears with my right hand, the sudden change unbalancing him. He lurched forward, overcommitted to resistance that was no longer there.

I pivoted left, using his momentum to swing him in a half-circle. The movement positioned the Shears' blades directly in line with something only I could see.

The keystone thread.

Through Thread Sight, it blazed like a rope of molten gold—the original contract that anchored Vane's entire structure of stolen power. It connected him to his first victim, the foundation upon which fifteen years of fraud had been built. Every other thread branched from this one. Every stolen marriage bond, every liquidated life, every murdered spouse traced back to this single point of origin.

I closed the Shears' blades with my left hand.

Scissor-cut motion.

The blades sliced through the thread.

The world fractured into gold.

The severed ends of the keystone thread recoiled like cables under tension—the upper end striking Vane in the chest with enough force to stagger him, the lower end snapping away into fog toward wherever his first victim's remains lay buried.

Vane released the Shears entirely. They fell to the stone floor with a clatter that seemed impossibly loud in the sudden silence.

Then the cascade began.

Every other thread connected to Vane started to glow brighter. Pulsing. Accelerating rhythm. Golden marriage bonds flared white-hot. Silver debt threads turned red. Black coercion cords began to smoke.

The threads vibrated, emitting a high-pitched sound like overstressed metal.

Then they began to snap.

One. Two. Five. Ten. Dozens breaking simultaneously—loose ends whipping backward like severed suspension cables, seeking anchors that no longer existed. Dead sources. Empty spaces where people used to be. Finding none, they dissolved into sparks of wasted equity.

The sound was glass shattering underwater, high-pitched and wrong.

Vane dropped to his knees, both hands clutching his chest.

Ink-black necrosis bloomed where the keystone thread had been severed—a starburst of darkness spreading outward like rot through wet parchment. The veins climbed his neck in branches, crawled across his jaw, reached the corners of his eyes. His skin stretched thin over bones that seemed to be shrinking beneath.

His sandy blonde hair bleached white in seconds. The colour drained from roots to tips, then the white dulled to grey. Patches began falling, loose strands drifting to the stone around him.

"Please." His voice cracked on the word. He raised his head, meeting my eyes. The charming warmth was gone, replaced by raw terror and confusion. "I was correcting an inefficiency..."

Blood leaked from the corners of his eyes—dark red against skin that had gone translucent, showing the network of black veins beneath like a second, dying circulatory system. More blood dripped from his nostrils, pooling on stone already wet from the Border Realm's perpetual damp.

I took one step backward.

This was binding sickness. Terminal stage. Twenty years of stolen power trying to return to its sources simultaneously, finding only corpses and empty spaces where people used to be. The magical energy had become poison with nowhere to drain.

Behind Vane, the twelve warding stones surrounding Clara's circle dimmed simultaneously—their glow fading from bright white to dark grey. The invisible barrier between them disappeared.

Clara stood uncertainly. Took one tentative step forward, then another. She stepped out of the circle and off the altar platform.

Frost's ice wall cracked and shattered, fragments falling like dropped glass and dissolving before they hit the ground. He moved toward the altar with long strides, reaching Clara in moments and catching her elbow as she swayed.

I crouched and lifted the Severing Shears from where they had fallen.

They were surprisingly heavy—iron and age making them dense despite their delicate appearance. Still warm but no longer glowing. Evidence. Material witness to what had just happened.

I stood, cradling the artifact against my chest. My hands shook with adrenaline, and I had to consciously steady them.

Vane had collapsed forward onto his hands, bracing against stone. His breathing came in wet gasps. His body had begun to look hollow, as if the bones themselves were dissolving.

He raised his head slightly. His mouth worked, trying to form words.

"Please." The word was barely audible. "I was... I didn't..."

I said nothing.

There was nothing to say. No legal argument. No procedural objection. No appeal to file. Just a man dying of the contracts he'd broken, the oaths he'd violated, the lives he'd stolen.

Around us, the Border Realm began to destabilise. The fog pressed closer. Architecture phased more rapidly, multiple eras flickering past in moments rather than minutes. The ground beneath my feet shifted from stone to earth to something that felt like water.

"We need to leave." Duan's voice cut through the chaos. "Now. The realm is rejecting him. When his wards collapse completely, this whole area becomes unstable."

Miller appeared at my elbow. "Can he walk?"

I looked at Vane again. His arms trembled with the effort of holding himself upright. Black veins had spread to his eyes, turning the whites grey.

"No."

"Then we leave him." Frost spoke from Clara's position, supporting her weight with one arm around her shoulders. His voice was steady, but something in his expression suggested the words cost him. "He violated too many oaths. Broke too many bonds. The realm itself is executing him."

The fog swirled around Vane's prone form, condensing until he was partially obscured. The ground beneath him rippled more dramatically than the surrounding floor, portions becoming transparent to show void beneath. Not empty space. *Void.* The grey nothing that existed under reality, pressing upward to claim what it was owed.

"Inspector..." Halloway rumbled from near the entrance. "Portal coordinates. We need to move."

The team converged. Halloway at point, positioning his massive frame near the doorway. Duan pulled out a small brass compass, the needle spinning before settling on a direction that had nothing to do with magnetic north. Miller kept his hand on my elbow, steadying me though I hadn't realised I was swaying.

Green closed her laptop and tucked it under one arm. Pip scrambled up my coat from where he'd taken shelter during the fighting, reclaiming his position on my shoulder.

"Leaving now, yes?" His voice was higher than usual. "Excellent. I've had quite enough of this realm."

Clara walked between Frost and Duan. Frost had one arm around her shoulders, supporting perhaps a third of her weight. Her feet moved, but her eyes stared straight ahead without focusing. Her face was blank, etched with the emptiness of someone whose mind had retreated from reality to protect itself.

I fell into formation, Miller on my left, Green behind me. The Severing Shears remained clutched against my chest.

We moved into fog that pressed against my face like damp gauze, tasting of rain and ashes.

Behind us, Vane screamed.

A scream that stripped the humanity from his throat—raw, wet, tearing. Rage and despair and physical agony compressed into one long note that cut through fog and distorted architecture.

I halted. Turned to look back.

The fog had swallowed everything. No chapel. No altar. No Vane. Only grey pressing in from all sides.

The scream rose in pitch, climbing toward frequencies that made my teeth ache.

Then stopped.

Sharp as a severed thread.

Miller pulled my elbow, gentle but insistent. "Come on."

I turned away from where Julian Vane had been and followed my team into the grey.

The Border Realm fought us every step.

Thirty meters became thirty miles in terms of difficulty. The ground shifted without warning—stone to earth to something soft and yielding that tried to swallow my feet. The fog moved in spirals, pulling in directions that had nothing to do with wind. Sound distorted. Duan's footsteps echoed before they landed. Frost's breathing seemed to come from somewhere behind me when he walked ahead.

The temperature fluctuated in pockets—warmth giving way to freezing cold, each shift disorienting my body's attempts to calibrate.

"Structure ahead," Duan called. "Twenty meters."

The fog parted reluctantly, revealing something that shouldn't exist in this dimension—black marble floor, floating chandeliers, the familiar oppressive architecture of the Obsidian Hall.

Duke of Ash was waiting.

He stood at the boundary between realms, tall and elegant in formal evening wear despite the hour. His ancient red eyes tracked our approach with the patience of something that had existed since before England had a name.

"The breach is sealed," he said as Frost crossed the threshold. "Your adversary's wards have collapsed entirely. The instability will spread for approximately three hours before the realm stabilises."

Frost inclined his head. "My thanks."

"The thanks belong to Miss Blackwell." Duke of Ash's attention shifted to me. "A Null severing a keystone contract using the Severing Shears. I have not witnessed such an... elegant solution in four centuries."

I didn't feel elegant. I felt exhausted, shaking, covered in fog-moisture and the grime of the Border

Realm. But I managed a nod that might have passed for acknowledgment.

Clara's knees buckled.

Frost caught her before she hit the marble, lowering her gently to sit on the floor. Her eyes had finally focused—but what they focused on was something none of us could see. Her hands gripped Frost's coat with desperate strength, and when she opened her mouth, the sound that emerged was a sob.

I dropped to my knees beside her.

"Clara." I reached for her hands, covered them with mine. "Clara, you're safe. We got you out. He can't hurt you anymore."

She looked at me. Recognition flickered—then crumbled into tears.

"I believed him." The words came out broken. "I believed everything. The romance. The understanding. The—" She couldn't finish. Her whole body shook with sobs that had been building since the moment she understood what Vane intended.

I pulled her against me, wrapping my arms around her shoulders, letting her cry into my coat. Over her head, I met Frost's eyes.

He looked as exhausted as I felt. But something in his expression suggested the exhaustion was worth it.

"Let's get her home," I said quietly.

Duke of Ash gestured toward a section of wall. A doorway appeared—not the portal to the Border

Realm, but something more mundane. A corridor that led to normal London, to streets and buildings and air that didn't taste of ash and broken contracts.

We helped Clara to her feet. She could walk now, though she leaned heavily on my arm. The sobs had quieted to shaking breaths, but her grip on my coat never loosened.

The team moved through the doorway in formation. Halloway first, scanning for threats that didn't exist in a quiet Mayfair street. Duan and Miller flanking. Green bringing up the rear with the Severing Shears wrapped in her coat.

Pip remained on my shoulder, silent for once.

The night air hit my face—cold, clean, smelling of rain and distant traffic. Real London. Mundane London. The city that continued existing regardless of what happened in the spaces between.

Halloway's M.O.P. vehicle waited at the curb.

I helped Clara into the back seat, sliding in beside her. She immediately curled against me, seeking contact, seeking safety. Her strawberry blonde hair was matted with fog-moisture and tears.

Frost climbed in on her other side. Duan took the driver's seat. The vehicle pulled away from the Mayfair address, leaving the Obsidian Hall behind.

The streets were empty at this hour. London slept, unaware that a predator had just been removed from its hidden population. Unaware that a woman had nearly died in a dimension that shouldn't exist. Unaware of anything except its own comfortable mundanity.

Clara's breathing eventually steadied against my shoulder.

"Is he dead?" she whispered.

"Yes."

"Good." The word held no satisfaction. Only exhaustion. "I'm glad. Is that wrong?"

"No." I tightened my arm around her. "That's not wrong at all."

She was quiet for a long moment. Then: "I'm sorry. For not listening. For believing him instead of you."

"You don't need to apologise."

"I do." She pulled back enough to look at me, eyes red-rimmed and devastated but finally present. "You tried to warn me. You tried to protect me. And I chose romance over reality because I wanted so badly for something to be true."

My throat tightened. "Clara—"

"Let me finish." She took a shaky breath. "I chose badly. But you came for me anyway. You broke laws and crossed dimensions and fought a monster with a pair of scissors because I was too stupid to see what was right in front of me."

"You weren't stupid. You were hopeful. There's a difference."

"Is there?"

I thought of Grimsby. Of my father's contract. Of all the times I'd wanted to believe the system could be reformed from within, could deliver justice through proper channels, could protect people like Clara without requiring someone to burn it down from outside.

"Yes," I said finally. "Hope isn't stupidity. It's just... vulnerable. And predators know how to exploit vulnerability."

Clara was quiet for a long moment.

"Okay," she said finally. "Okay."

She leaned against my shoulder again, and I let her. Outside the window, London passed in streaks of streetlight and shadow.

We were going home.

Whatever came next—the questions, the tribunals, the consequences of operating without authorisation—we would face it together.

For now, that was enough.

Chapter 15: The Weight of Winning

The flat smelled of cold tea and abandoned worry when we finally climbed the stairs.

Clara's door stood open—she'd left in a hurry for the gala, hours ago, a lifetime ago. Her vanity mirror reflected the hallway light, showing scattered makeup brushes and the cream-coloured dress she'd considered before choosing the pastel gown now ruined by Border Realm fog and tears.

I guided her to the sofa, and she sat without resistance. Her eyes had gone unfocused again, retreating somewhere I couldn't follow.

Frost stood in the doorway, uncertainty visible in the set of his shoulders. He looked wrong in my flat—too tall for the ceiling, too formal for the faded floral wallpaper, too contained for a space that had absorbed two years of Clara's chaotic warmth and my stubborn practicality.

"I should go," he said. "The seal requires monitoring. Augusta's coverage is temporary."

"Of course."

He didn't move. His hand rose toward his waistcoat pocket, reaching for the pocket watch, then stopped. The gesture aborted halfway.

"The Tribunal will convene within seventy-two hours," he said instead. "The Council cannot ignore what happened. There will be questions about jurisdiction, authorisation, the manner of Vane's death."

"I know."

"I will testify on your behalf. My team as well. What we witnessed—"

"Frost." I met his eyes across the cramped space. "Go. Take care of the seal. We'll handle the rest."

Something flickered in his expression—gratitude, perhaps, or something more complicated. He inclined his head once, turned, and descended the stairs. The front door closed behind him with a quiet click.

I listened to the silence he left behind.

Then I went to make tea, because that was what you did when the world had broken and you didn't know how to fix it.

The kettle was boiling when Miller arrived.

He appeared in the kitchen doorway without announcement, still wearing the civilian clothes from the rescue operation. His wire-rimmed glasses reflected the overhead light, hiding his eyes.

"Duan dropped me off," he said. "Thought you might need someone who isn't emotionally invested."

"And you're not emotionally invested?"

"I'm a homicide detective who just watched a serial killer die of magical backlash in an alternate dimension." He moved to the counter, pulling down two cups with the familiarity of someone who'd made tea in stranger circumstances. "I'm professionally invested. Different thing."

He prepared the tea with efficient movements—kettle, cups, leaves, timing. The ritual grounded something in me that had been floating loose since the chapel.

We sat at the kitchen table, hands wrapped around cups too hot to drink comfortably. The heat was the point. Something to feel that wasn't the memory of Vane's black veins spreading, his hair turning white, his voice cracking on words that meant nothing.

"You did what was necessary," Miller said. "For the record."

"I used contract law as a murder weapon." My voice came out flat. "Successfully."

"You stopped a serial killer who was using marriage contracts to drain people dry. The method doesn't change the outcome."

"The method is everything, Detective. That's the problem with the magical legal system." I stared into my tea, watching steam curl upward. "The tools work for anyone who knows how to use them. Vane exploited contracts to kill. I exploited contracts to kill Vane. We used identical mechanisms. Only intention differed."

Miller was quiet for a moment. Drank his tea. Set the cup down with careful precision.

"You gave him chances to stop. Multiple chances. He chose to continue."

"Did I?" I met his eyes. "Or did I create a situation where the only outcome was his death? Once that keystone thread was cut, the backlash was inevitable. I knew that. I did it anyway."

"Because it was the only way to save Clara and stop him from killing again." Miller's voice was firm, the tone of a man who'd spent twenty years making peace with necessary ugliness. "Intent matters, Miss Blackwell. You're not Vane."

"Tonight I was."

The words hung between us. Miller didn't argue. He understood better than most, the particular weight of doing terrible things for defensible reasons.

"The Tribunal will want to dissect every decision," he said finally. "They'll question your judgment, your methods, your authority to act. The conservative faction will push for prosecution. Contract fraud. Vigilantism. Possibly murder."

"I know."

"Frost will testify. So will I. Duan, Halloway, Green—we all saw what happened. Clara can speak to Vane's intentions, the trap he set, what would have happened if you hadn't intervened."

"And if that's not enough?"

Miller stood, taking his empty cup to the sink. "Then you'll need better lawyers than the ones who prosecuted Vane's victims for fifteen years."

He turned to face me, leaning against the counter with his arms crossed.

"Get some sleep, Miss Blackwell. Tomorrow the questions start. You'll want to be sharp for them."

"Thank you, Detective. For everything tonight."

"Don't thank me yet." He moved toward the door. "We broke about seventeen regulations and possibly a few laws. If this goes badly, we're all answering questions."

"Then I'll make sure it doesn't go badly."

Miller's mouth twitched—not quite a smile. "That's what I'm counting on."

He let himself out. The flat door closed quietly behind him.

I sat alone at the kitchen table, tea cooling in my hands, and thought about contracts and consequences and the thin line between justice and revenge.

Clara slept on the sofa, wrapped in the old quilt she'd brought from her previous life.

I'd tried to move her to her bedroom, but she'd gripped my hand with sudden fierce strength and whispered "please don't leave me alone." So I'd brought the quilt, made more tea she didn't drink, and sat in the armchair across from her until her breathing finally steadied into something like rest.

She looked younger when she slept. The careful composure she'd learned to maintain—the bright smiles and cheerful deflections that kept people from seeing how much she'd lost—all of it smoothed away. What remained was a woman who'd been hurt too many times and had just narrowly escaped being hurt again.

I should have seen it sooner. Should have recognised Vane for what he was the moment Clara mentioned his name. Should have found some way to make her listen that didn't require waiting until she was trapped in a warding circle in an alternate dimension.

Should have. Could have. Didn't.

The self-recrimination was familiar. I'd worn grooves in these thoughts over the years—every client I couldn't help, every case I lost, every predatory contract that slipped through loopholes I'd tried to close. The weight of inadequacy was an old companion.

But Clara was alive. Traumatized, devastated, facing a recovery that would take months or years—but alive. And Vane was dead, his victims' stolen power returning to whatever void claimed energy without living anchors.

I'd take that trade. Every time.

Pip emerged from his filing cabinet nest around three in the morning. He climbed onto the arm of my chair, settling into a seated position with his small hands folded.

"You should sleep," he said quietly.

"Can't."

"Can't or won't?"

"Does it matter?"

He was silent for a moment, amber eyes reflecting the dim light from the street below.

"The brownie network is already spreading word of what happened," he said. "By dawn, every household servant in supernatural London will know that Julian Vane is dead and a working-class Scribe killed him."

"Is that good or bad?"

"Both." His ears twitched. "The exploited will see hope. The exploiters will see threat. The Council will see a problem that requires management." He looked at me directly. "You've become visible, Miss Blackwell. That changes everything."

"I've always been visible. The M.O.P. knew about my work for years."

"They knew about a small-practise solicitor helping contract-broken individuals navigate legal loopholes. Irritating but containable." Pip's voice held no judgment, only assessment. "Now they know about a Null who can sever keystone contracts and bring down fifteen-year conspiracy networks. That's different. That's dangerous."

I thought about Augusta's dress, her etiquette instructions, her warning about standing on Frost's correct side. She'd seen this coming. Seen that tonight would change my position whether I wanted it to or not.

"What do you recommend?"

"Survive the Tribunal. Establish the narrative before your enemies can. Make yourself too useful to eliminate and too costly to antagonize." Pip's ears flattened slightly. "And perhaps consider whether continuing to operate from a cramped Clerkenwell office above a kebab shop projects the appropriate image for someone who just killed an aristocratic serial murderer."

"I like this office."

"I know. That's the problem."

Clara stirred on the sofa, making a small sound of distress. I was at her side before conscious thought, smoothing hair back from her forehead, murmuring reassurances I wasn't sure she could hear.

She settled again, one hand gripping the quilt's edge.

I returned to the armchair.

"The Tribunal will convene within seventy-two hours," I said. "We need to prepare testimony, organise evidence, anticipate the prosecution's arguments."

"I've already begun compiling relevant precedents." Pip climbed down from the chair arm. "Emergency doctrine, defensive nullification, the 1847 ruling on contract fraud cessation. The legal framework exists to justify your actions. Whether the Council chooses to acknowledge that framework is a political question, not a legal one."

"Then we need to make the political calculation favour acknowledgment."

"Yes." Pip paused at the filing cabinet. "Miss Blackwell. For what it's worth—you did the right thing tonight. The method was ugly. The outcome was necessary. I would rather work for someone who struggles with that distinction than someone who doesn't notice it exists."

He disappeared into his cabinet before I could respond.

I sat in the dark, watching Clara sleep, and waited for dawn.

Morning arrived grey and reluctant, London's winter light filtering through windows I hadn't thought to curtain.

Clara woke slowly, confusion giving way to memory giving way to something that looked like grief. She sat up, quilt pooling around her waist, and stared at nothing for a long moment.

"It wasn't a nightmare," she said finally.

"No."

"He really was going to kill me."

"Yes."

She was quiet. Processing. Her hands moved to touch the gold necklace she still wore—Vane's gift, the chain he'd placed around her throat at the gala—and flinched away as if burned.

"I need to take this off." Her voice cracked. "I can't—I need—"

I crossed to the sofa, sitting beside her. "Let me."

The clasp was delicate, expensive, designed to look simple while actually being complex. My fingers found the mechanism after a moment's fumbling. The chain came free.

Clara let out a breath that shook her whole body.

"What do I do with it?"

"Whatever you want. Throw it away. Sell it. Melt it down." I set the necklace on the side table. "It's yours now. He can't take it back."

"Nothing is mine." She pulled the quilt tighter around her shoulders. "Everything I have came from somewhere else. The flat. The job. The—the magic I used to have before Eli took it." Her eyes found mine. "I don't even know who I am without someone else's context."

"You're Clara Vance. You survived a predatory marriage, rebuilt your life, and didn't let a second predator destroy you."

"I didn't survive. You survived for me."

"You held on long enough for help to arrive. That's survival."

She shook her head, but some of the desperate edge had left her expression. "I don't know how to do this. How to be okay after—after everything."

"You don't have to know yet." I squeezed her hand. "You just have to get through today. Then tomorrow. One day at a time until it gets easier."

"Does it get easier?"

I thought about my father's contract, signed when I was too young to understand what it meant. About the years of watching my mother struggle, then stop struggling, then disappear into the blankness of someone whose fight had been drained away. About Grimsby and the night I'd found his body and the questions I still couldn't answer.

"Different," I said finally. "It gets different. Whether that's easier depends on what you do with it."

Clara was quiet for a long moment. Then she reached out and pulled me into a hug—fierce, sudden, desperate.

"Thank you," she whispered against my shoulder. "For coming for me. For not giving up."

I held her and didn't say anything.

Some things didn't need words.

The rest of the day passed in a blur of practical necessities.

Green arrived mid-morning with the Severing Shears, now properly wrapped and documented as evidence. She also brought coffee, pastries, and a preliminary analysis of Vane's financial network that would take weeks to fully untangle.

"The cascade is still propagating," she said, spreading printouts across my desk. "Every contract he touched is destabilizing. Some will fail completely—the victims' estates may be able to recover assets. Others are too entangled with legitimate agreements. We'll need teams of Scribes working for months to sort it out."

"The victims' families?"

"The widows and widowers are being notified. Unofficially, for now—the Council hasn't authorised formal disclosure. But word is spreading." Green's purple hair had been re-tied into its usual ponytail, professional mask back in place despite the exhaustion beneath it. "You're going to have a lot of potential clients, Miss Blackwell."

The thought was overwhelming. Forty-three families, potentially. Forty-three cases of predatory contracts, stolen assets, murdered spouses. Even if half of them sought representation, I'd be working for years.

"One case at a time," I said.

"That's the only way to do it."

Duan and Halloway stopped by in the afternoon, officially to deliver updates on Border Realm stability, unofficially to check on Clara and offer support. They stayed for tea—Clara insisted, the ritual of hospitality giving her something to do with her hands—and the conversation carefully avoided anything to do with chapels or severed threads or men dying of their own broken oaths.

Miller called twice with questions about evidence chain of custody. Frost sent a message through official channels confirming the Tribunal date: seventy-two hours, as predicted. The Council wanted this resolved quickly, one way or another.

I spent the evening preparing.

The case file grew: witness statements, financial records, contract analyses, the complex legal argument for why what I'd done constituted emergency defence rather than premeditated murder. Pip retrieved precedents from storage with grim efficiency, his usual complaints about filing systems absent in the face of actual crisis.

Clara sat on the sofa with a cup of tea she never drank, watching me work. She'd showered, changed into comfortable clothes, eaten half a piece of toast that I'd practically forced on her. Small victories.

"Will they put you in prison?" she asked quietly.

I looked up from the brief I was drafting. "I don't know."

"That's not reassuring."

"I know." I set down my pen. "The Council has to balance several factors. Punishing me satisfies the conservative faction and reinforces their authority. But it also means acknowledging that their procedures failed catastrophically—that Vane operated for fifteen years because their system enabled him. Some of them would rather declare me a hero than admit that."

"And the others?"

"Would rather declare me a villain than admit anything at all."

Clara was quiet for a moment. "What happens to me if you go to prison?"

The question hit harder than I expected. I'd been so focused on the immediate crisis—survive tonight, survive the Tribunal, survive whatever came after—that I hadn't let myself think about the longer implications.

"Pip would help you," I said finally. "The office would continue. You'd have resources, connections, people who care about you."

"That's not what I asked."

"I know." I met her eyes. "I'm not planning to go to prison, Clara. But if I do—you'll be okay. I'll make sure of it."

She didn't look convinced. But she nodded and returned to staring at her cold tea.

Outside the window, London settled into evening. The kebab shop below did steady business, customers coming and going, lives continuing in comfortable ignorance of the magical world that existed alongside their own.

Somewhere in that city, forty-three families were learning that the deaths they'd mourned had been murders. That the system they'd trusted had failed them. That a working-class Scribe had done what the Council couldn't or wouldn't do.

The phone would ring eventually. It always did. And I would answer. Every time.

But first—the Tribunal. The questions. The political calculation that would determine whether I emerged as reformer or criminal.

I picked up my pen and returned to work. The brief wasn't going to write itself.

Chapter 16: The Tribunal

The Old Bailey looked different when you were walking to your own judgment.

I'd been in this building dozens of times—filing motions, reviewing evidence, representing clients who couldn't afford anyone else. The Portland stone and modern security checkpoints had become familiar. Comfortable, even, in the way that working spaces become comfortable through repetition.

None of that comfort remained as I followed Frost through the main entrance.

Clara walked beside me, her hand gripping mine with desperate strength. She'd insisted on coming, despite my arguments that she should rest, recover, let me face this alone. "You came for me," she'd said, the words brooking no argument. "I'm coming for you."

Pip rode her shoulder, unusually quiet. He'd spent the past three days compiling precedents, organizing testimony, preparing the legal framework for my defence. Now there was nothing left to do but watch it unfold.

We passed through corridors painted institutional cream, fluorescent lights buzzing overhead. Then the walls changed.

Painted plaster gave way to carved white stone. Modern fixtures disappeared, replaced by cold mage-lights that illuminated without warmth. The shift was seamless if you weren't watching for it—one moment courthouse, the next something else entirely.

The wards pulsed against my Null status. Static crawled across my skin, tasting of copper and ancient obligation. This space operated under different rules.

Frost stopped at a heavy wooden door twenty feet tall, carved with sigils I recognised from my training. The seal of the High Council.

"They'll focus on you," he said quietly. "The unauthorised action angle is easier than admitting the system failed. Answer truthfully but don't volunteer information they haven't asked for."

"I know how tribunals work."

"Not this one." He reached for the door. "This one was designed to make you submit."

The hinges moved without sound.

The chamber beyond was enormous.

Stone walls rose forty feet to a vaulted ceiling painted with scenes of magical justice—blindfolded figures weighing souls on golden scales, contract scrolls unfurling into binding light. The floor was polished black marble that reflected the mage-lights like still water.

At the far end, thirteen chairs arranged in a semicircle on an elevated platform. The High Council bench. Each seat bore a family crest carved into its back—ancient names that had governed supernatural London for centuries.

Nine of the chairs were occupied. Lady Augusta Stern sat in the center position, her silver hair severe against black judicial robes. Her expression when she saw me suggested she had anticipated this moment without welcoming it.

The gallery behind the central floor held perhaps fifty observers—M.O.P. officers in uniform, Scribe Guild representatives, aristocratic observers who'd come to witness the spectacle. At the end of one bench, I spotted Miller, Green, Halloway, and Duan seated together in civilian clothes. Unofficial support. Witnesses who knew what had actually happened.

A salt circle had been laid into the floor before the Council bench—the traditional boundary for testimony. I would stand inside it when I spoke, bound by ritual to speak truth within its confines.

Clara found a seat in the gallery, Pip still on her shoulder. She caught my eye and nodded once. Support without spectacle.

Augusta struck a silver gavel against the bench. The sound rang through the chamber like a bell, and all conversation ceased.

"This Tribunal is convened to address the matter of Julian Vane, deceased, and the actions taken by Metropolitan Occult Police personnel and civilian consultants in connection with said death." Her voice carried the weight of centuries of authority. "The Council will hear testimony, examine evidence, and render judgment according to supernatural law."

She paused, scanning the chamber with pale blue eyes that missed nothing.

"Scribes, activate your memory stones. Let the record show all who are present."

Four court reporters at desks flanking the chamber touched small crystals to their foreheads. The stones began to glow faint blue, pulsing in rhythm with breathing. Recording everything.

Augusta gestured toward a podium to the Council's left. "Prosecutor, present the charges."

A middle-aged man in formal robes rose from the front gallery—Crown counsel I recognised from previous proceedings, a specialist in contract law violations. He positioned himself at the podium with deliberate care.

"The High Council charges that Imogen Blackwell, certified Scribe, did willfully employ unauthorised nullification magic in violation of Codex provisions regarding contract sanctity. Further, that she acted beyond the scope of her professional authority by participating in vigilante action that resulted in the death of Julian Vane, citizen of supernatural London."

He lifted his documents, voice carrying clearly.

"Miss Blackwell's actions, while perhaps well-intentioned, undermine the fundamental principles upon which our society operates. If Scribes may unilaterally decide which contracts have validity, the entire system collapses. If civilian consultants may act as judge, jury, and executioner, law becomes meaningless. The Council must determine whether emergency circumstances justify these violations, or whether Miss Blackwell must face consequences for her actions."

He turned to face me directly.

"The charges include contract fraud, unauthorised practise of nullification magic, and complicity in the death of Julian Vane. The prosecution requests formal censure, revocation of Scribe certification, and potential imprisonment pending the Council's assessment of severity."

The words landed like physical blows. Revocation. Imprisonment. Everything I'd built, everything Grimsby had taught me, everything I'd fought for—all of it balanced on whatever judgment this chamber reached.

Augusta inclined her head. "Miss Blackwell. Enter the circle."

I walked across the black marble floor, footsteps echoing in the sudden silence. The salt circle waited, gleaming white against dark stone. I stepped across its boundary and felt the ritual attention settle over me like a weight—the magic that would ensure truth, that would know if I lied.

"You have heard the charges," Augusta said. "How do you respond?"

I took a breath. Steadied myself.

"I acknowledge that I employed nullification magic without prior Council authorisation. I acknowledge that I participated in an unauthorised rescue operation that resulted in Julian Vane's death." My voice came out steady, professional. The voice I'd learned in courtrooms, arguing for clients who had no one else. "I deny that these actions constitute fraud against the magical contract system. I deny that Vane's death was murder."

"Explain."

"Julian Vane was in the process of murdering Clara Vance when I intervened. He had trapped her in a warding circle, was preparing to sever her life threads using the Severing Shears—an artifact supposedly destroyed centuries ago. Official channels had failed to stop him. The High Council denied our warrant request. The M.O.P. had no jurisdiction in the Border Realm. The only options were intervention or allowing another victim to die."

I met Augusta's eyes directly.

"I chose intervention. The nullification magic I employed targeted the keystone contract anchoring Vane's entire fraudulent network—a contract obtained through deception that violated consent requirements. When that contract failed, the cascading obligations he'd built on fraudulent foundation collapsed, causing binding sickness that resulted in his death."

"You admit to engineering his death."

"I admit to stopping him from killing Clara Vance. The binding sickness was consequence of his own violated oaths, not my action. I removed a foundation built on fraud. The collapse was inevitable once that foundation was exposed."

The prosecutor stepped forward. "A distinction without difference, Miss Blackwell. You knew breaking the keystone contract would kill him. You did it anyway. That constitutes murder."

"It constitutes the enforcement of a contract's natural conclusion."

I hadn't planned the words—hadn't rehearsed or consulted precedent or run the argument past Pip's encyclopaedic knowledge of procedural law. I was arguing from first principles in a courtroom I had no formal standing to address, making a case that would have required advocacy certification to present in any legitimate proceeding.

But the salt circle didn't care about certification. It cared about truth. And every word I'd spoken had landed without resistance, the ritual magic confirming what the professional hierarchy refused to acknowledge: I was doing a barrister's work. I had been doing it since the moment I'd stepped into Frost's investigation and started building a case instead of reviewing one.

Augusta's gaze held mine for a fraction longer than procedure required. Whatever she saw there, she didn't comment on it.

Murmurs rippled through the gallery. Augusta's gavel struck once, demanding silence.

"The Council will hear testimony from other witnesses before deliberation," she announced. "Inspector Frost. Approach."

Frost entered the salt circle with military precision, positioning himself beside me without acknowledging the proximity. His formal testimony voice emerged—clipped, factual, stripped of personal inflection.

"The Metropolitan Occult Police investigation confirmed Julian Vane as the perpetrator of at least four murders spanning fifteen years. His methodology involved predatory marriage contracts, systematic soul-equity extraction, and the use of the Severing Shears to sever binding threads prematurely. Miss Blackwell's analysis was instrumental in identifying these patterns."

"And the unauthorised rescue operation?" Augusta asked.

"I organised and led that operation." Frost's voice didn't waver. "Miss Blackwell participated at my request. The decision to proceed without authorisation was mine."

"You abandoned your duty to the Void seal."

"I delegated monitoring to Lady Augusta and reinforced the wards before departing. The seal remained stable throughout the operation."

"You risked catastrophic failure for the sake of one civilian."

Frost was silent for a moment. When he spoke, his voice had lost some of its formal distance.

"I risked appropriately. Julian Vane's murders would have continued, creating a pattern of exploitation that threatened not just individual victims but the entire social structure's stability. His scheme, left unchecked, would have eventually forced Council intervention far more disruptive than my temporary absence." He paused. "Additionally, Miss Blackwell had placed herself in danger to pursue this investigation. I was not willing to abandon her."

The admission hung in the chamber's still air. Several Council members exchanged glances.

Augusta's expression remained unreadable.

"The Council acknowledges your strategic reasoning. However, we cannot condone abandoning the Void seal under any circumstances." She lifted a document. "You will be formally censured for dereliction of duty. This censure will be noted in your service record but will not result in loss of rank or authority. You are credited with preventing a larger catastrophe through your actions, even as you are condemned for the method employed."

Frost inclined his head. "I accept the Council's judgment."

He stepped out of the salt circle, returned to his position at the evidence table. His eyes found mine briefly—a flicker of reassurance—before his attention returned to formal neutrality.

The testimony continued for hours.

Miller presented the financial analysis—shell companies, fraudulent transfers, the systematic pattern of death following Vane's "consulting services." His wire-rimmed glasses reflected the mage-lights as he laid out evidence that made even the conservative Council members shift uncomfortably.

Duan testified about the Border Realm operation, the chapel's configuration, Vane's defensive wards. Her voice remained steady as she described finding Clara in the warding circle, the moment when intervention became the only option.

Green provided technical analysis of the contract cascade—how Vane's network had been structured, why the keystone thread's severance triggered system-wide collapse. Her purple hair seemed to glow in the chamber's strange light as she explained mechanisms that made several Council members look slightly ill.

Clara testified last.

She entered the salt circle with visible trembling, but her voice held steady as she described her marriage to Elias Thorne under his assumed name, the slow drain of her magic over years, the trap that had closed around her at the Obsidian Hall. When she spoke about the warding circle—about understanding, finally, what Vane intended—her composure cracked.

"He told me it would be quick," she said, tears streaming down her face. "He told me I wouldn't suffer long. Like that was supposed to be comfort. Like I should be grateful he wasn't planning to make it hurt."

The gallery had gone absolutely silent.

"Imogen came for me." Clara's voice strengthened. "She came for me when no one else could, when the system you built failed to protect me. If that's a crime, then your system is broken. Because the only criminal in that chapel was the man who was going to kill me."

She stepped out of the circle and returned to her seat. Pip climbed onto her shoulder, pressing against her neck in small comfort.

Augusta called for deliberation.

The Council members withdrew to a chamber behind the bench. The gallery erupted into whispered conversation—speculation, assessment, the electric buzz of people who knew they were witnessing something significant without being certain what it meant.

Frost appeared at my elbow. "You did well."

"I told the truth inside a circle designed to ensure truth-telling. That's not difficult."

"It is when the truth threatens powerful interests." He glanced toward the door where the Council had disappeared. "Augusta will argue for leniency. She's conservative, but she's pragmatic—she can read political currents. The reform faction will support us. The question is whether they have enough votes."

"And if they don't?"

"Then we find other ways to continue the work."

I looked at him—at the formal posture that had softened slightly over the past weeks, at the pale grey eyes that held something more complicated than professional assessment.

"Thank you," I said. "For testifying. For the censure you accepted."

"The censure costs me nothing material. They cannot afford to lose me because I anchor the seal." His mouth twitched. "Pride is a luxury I cannot afford. Duty matters. Pride does not."

Before I could respond, the chamber door opened.

The Council returned.

Augusta resumed her central position, her expression giving nothing away. The other members arranged themselves on either side—conservatives to her right, reformists to her left, moderates scattered between. The fault lines were visible to anyone who knew how to look.

"The Council has deliberated," Augusta announced. "The following determinations have been reached."

She lifted a document—formal script on heavy parchment.

"First: Regarding the charges against Miss Imogen Blackwell. The Council finds that her actions, while technically in violation of Codex provisions, were taken in emergency circumstances that justify deviation from standard procedure. The nullification magic she employed targeted a fraudulent contract obtained through deception. The resulting death was consequence of the perpetrator's own violations, not direct action by Miss Blackwell."

My breath caught.

"Miss Blackwell will receive formal censure for operating beyond the scope of her professional authority. This censure will be noted in her certification record but will not result in revocation or imprisonment. She is credited with preventing murder and exposing systematic failures in Council oversight."

The gallery erupted. Voices raised in protest from the conservative section, murmurs of approval from elsewhere. Augusta's gavel struck three times before order returned.

"Second: The Council acknowledges that Julian Vane's crimes were enabled by gaps in our procedures. Lord Ashford has proposed comprehensive reforms to prevent future predators from exploiting similar loopholes."

Lord Ashford rose from his Council seat, holding prepared documents. "Mandatory Scribe review of all marriage contracts containing power-sharing clauses. Standardised protections against soul-equity liquidation. Prohibition of contract modifications that accelerate extraction beyond originally agreed terms. Debt-binding limitations to prevent working-class supernatural beings from being trapped in permanent servitude."

A conservative Lord—Blackwood, ancient family—rose in opposition. "These reforms would require the Council to insert itself into private contractual arrangements of families who have managed their own affairs for centuries. One predator does not justify burning the orchard."

"Twenty-three dead women in fifteen years," Lord Ashford shot back. "How many orchards must burn before we admit the soil is poisoned?"

The debate continued for two hours—political maneuvering that would have made Parliament look efficient. Conservative members raised objections with patient condescension. Progressive members countered with moral arguments and victim testimony. The gallery watched, rapt, as the future of supernatural contract law was argued in formal phrases and barely concealed contempt.

Finally, a moderate Council member proposed compromise legislation—mandatory Scribe review for contracts exceeding soul-equity thresholds, increased penalties for documented fraud, standardised dissolution clauses in marriage contracts. Watered down from the original proposals, but something.

Augusta called for vote.

"All in favour of the compromise reforms?"

Seven hands rose.

"Opposed?"

Five hands.

"The reforms pass." Augusta struck her gavel. "Legislation will be drafted within thirty days and implemented within six months."

The Tribunal addressed victim compensation next.

Clara's name was called. She stood slowly, still trembling.

Augusta's voice softened fractionally. "Miss Vance. The Council acknowledges the harm you suffered through Julian Vane's manipulation and the exploitation you endured in your previous marriage. We offer access to healing services specializing in magical and psychological trauma, funded through the High Council's discretionary budget. Additionally, you are awarded reparations from Julian Vane's liquidated estate in the amount of fifteen thousand pounds."

She paused.

"We recognise that no monetary compensation can restore what was taken. This offer is acknowledgment of harm done, not equivalence of value."

Clara nodded once, sat down. Her hands shook holding the envelope they'd given her.

Other victims' families were called in sequence—widows and widowers who'd lost spouses to Vane's predation. Each received similar offers, reparations varying based on documented damages. The procession of names created a litany of harm that the chamber had to witness, had to acknowledge, could no longer pretend didn't exist.

Finally, Augusta struck her gavel three times.

"The case of Julian Vane is officially closed. The Council rules that Vane acted alone in his criminal enterprise. His death resulted from binding sickness caused by his own fraudulent contracts' collapse. No further investigation is warranted."

The massive Tribunal Ledger on Augusta's bench began to glow. Words appeared in golden script, recording the judgment permanently.

Case sealed. No appeals. No additional inquiry.

I felt Pip's claws dig into my shoulder—he'd moved from Clara at some point during the proceedings. We both understood what that ruling meant. Whoever had given Vane the Severing Shears, whoever might have helped him acquire forbidden artifacts, whoever potentially orchestrated the larger conspiracy—none of it would be investigated officially.

The Council wanted closure more than truth.

"This Tribunal is concluded."

The chamber filled with motion—gallery attendees clustering in groups, Council members descending to speak with faction representatives, M.O.P. officers moving toward exits. I sat in my seat, exhausted, while people flowed past.

Clara leaned against my shoulder, eyes closed. We'd won. Partially. Insufficiently. But more than I'd expected.

Augusta descended from the bench and approached. The gallery observers gave her wide berth, recognizing that whatever conversation was about to happen wasn't meant for them.

"Miss Blackwell. Walk with me."

It wasn't a request.

I followed her to an alcove off the main chamber—private, warded against eavesdropping. She turned to face me, and for the first time I saw something other than cold calculation in her expression.

"I watched my nephew choose relationship over absolute duty," she said. "I spent thirty years teaching him that such choices lead to catastrophe. Yet his choice prevented murders and exposed procedural failures I had chosen not to address."

Her pale eyes held mine.

"You were correct about the Council's procedural gaps. I was wrong to delay investigation. That admission costs me politically, but accuracy matters more than comfort."

I didn't know how to respond. Augusta wasn't offering friendship—barely offering alliance. But she was acknowledging error, which for someone of her generation and status was revolution.

"The conservative faction will not forgive this easily," she continued. "Baroness Fell and her allies view you as a dangerous radical who must be eliminated. Expect retaliation disguised as legitimate business—contract disputes filed against your clients, complaints to the Scribes Guild, social pressure designed to make your practise impossible."

"I expected that."

"Good. Then you understand the cost of visibility. You cannot operate quietly anymore. Every action will be scrutinized, every choice questioned. This Tribunal made you a symbol, and symbols are targets."

She turned to leave, then paused.

"One more thing. My nephew has been... persistent in his inquiries regarding your recovery. I suggest you resolve that ambiguity before it affects his efficiency."

She walked away before I could respond, robes sweeping marble.

I stood processing what she'd said. Frost had asked about me. Multiple times. Persistently.

Footsteps approached from behind. I turned to find Frost standing at careful distance, hands clasped behind his back.

"Miss Blackwell."

"Inspector."

We stood in silence for a moment.

"The reforms passed," he said finally. "Insufficient but meaningful."

"Yes."

"The case closure was political necessity rather than truth."

"I know."

Another silence.

"I have not stopped investigating who provided Vane with the Severing Shears," he said quietly. "The Tribunal ruled no further inquiry necessary, but my curiosity remains active."

"Officially or unofficially?"

"The distinction seems less relevant than results."

I almost smiled. Almost.

"Thank you for your testimony," I said. "The censure—"

"—was symbolic punishment the Council required to maintain authority. They cannot afford to lose me. The reprimand costs me nothing material."

"It costs you pride."

Something flickered in his pale grey eyes. "Pride is luxury I cannot afford. Duty matters. Pride does not."

He inclined his head—formal gesture of departure.

"If you require M.O.P. resources for future cases, my door remains open. Officially as consultant relationship. Unofficially as..." He paused. "Colleague who respects your work."

He left before I could respond, walking toward the exit with perfect military precision.

I returned to Clara and Pip.

"Come on," I said quietly. "Let's go home."

We emerged from the courthouse into grey London afternoon. Rain threatened but didn't fall. Traffic noise and pedestrian chaos surrounded us—ordinary city continuing exactly as before, unaware of what had just happened beneath its feet.

The contrast was jarring. The Tribunal chamber's formality, the political maneuvering, the literal judgment of my worthiness—all of it occurring while mundane humans went about their lives entirely oblivious.

Clara took my arm as we walked toward the Tube station. Pip rode my shoulder, muttering about insufficient reforms and political cowardice and how seven votes was barely a majority.

"Pip," I said quietly. "We survived. That's enough for today."

He subsided into grumpy silence.

The Tube was crowded, forcing us to stand pressed against other commuters. No one looked at us. No one cared that we'd just participated in supernatural proceedings that might reshape magical contract law for generations.

We were invisible again. Ordinary.

It felt like relief.

Back at the flat, I unlocked the door to find everything exactly as we'd left it. Cluttered desk, overflowing files, Pip's meticulously organised records. The familiar mess of my professional life.

Clara went immediately to the kitchen, started making tea. The ritual grounding her.

Pip climbed down from my shoulder, moved to his cushion near the radiator.

I stood at my window overlooking the street, watching the kebab shop below, the pedestrians passing, the mundane world that existed alongside and ignorant of the magical one.

The phone rang.

I stared at it for a moment, then crossed to my desk and picked up.

"Blackwell and Vance, how may I help you?"

"Miss Blackwell?" Unfamiliar voice, female, working-class accent. "My name is Sarah Mitchell. I heard about the Tribunal today. About what you did for those victims. I... I have a contract problem. Predatory marriage agreement my sister signed before she died. The family is trying to claim her estate through debt-binding clauses and I can't afford legal representation and I don't know what to do..."

I pulled a notepad toward me, uncapped my pen.

"Tell me about the contract, Miss Mitchell. Start from the beginning."

While she talked, I took notes. Clara brought tea, set it on my desk without speaking. Pip climbed onto the desk, already pulling relevant precedent files from memory.

The work continued. One case at a time. One client at a time. Small victories and partial protections and insufficient remedies that were still better than nothing.

The Tribunal had been important. The reforms would help. The reparations mattered.

But none of it fixed the fundamental problem. The system was broken. The law enabled exploitation. Power protected predators.

And I was going to keep fighting it anyway, because someone had to, and apparently I was too stubborn to stop.

The phone would ring again. It always did.

And I would answer. Every time.

Chapter 17: New Foundations

The invitation arrived three days after the Tribunal.

I found it when I returned from Clerkenwell Market with fresh herbs for my Null-Ink preparation—a cream-coloured envelope propped against the office doorframe where someone had left it without knocking. The paper was heavy, expensive, the kind most people couldn't afford to use for grocery lists. The seal on the back was pressed wax bearing the Frost family crest, frost crystals and geometric precision that probably doubled as a minor authentication charm.

Pip noticed it before I did. "That's Frost family cardstock. I can smell the ward-work from here."

Inside, the handwriting was unmistakably Frost's. Controlled script, every letter perfectly formed, the same precision he brought to case files and official documents.

Miss Blackwell,

I request your presence at Ashwood Manor on Thursday afternoon for consultation regarding ongo-

ing matters. If this is agreeable, a car will collect you at two o'clock.

Respectfully,

Lord Nathaniel Frost

No flowery language. No social pleasantries about hoping I was well. Just a straightforward request in the same tone he'd use for summoning a witness.

Except he'd written it by hand instead of having a secretary type it. That meant something, though I wasn't entirely sure what.

"Consultation," Pip read, peering over my shoulder. "At Ashwood Manor. Interesting venue for official business. Usually one conducts consultations in an office, not a Georgian fortress."

"It says consultation."

"It says his house. His private residence." Pip's amber eyes reflected the afternoon light. "That's personal, Miss Blackwell."

Clara appeared in the doorway, teacup in hand. She'd been doing better lately—the trembling in her hands finally gone, colour returning to her cheeks. The nightmares still came, but less frequently now, and she'd started humming again while she organised files.

"Are you going?" she asked.

I traced the embossed seal with one finger. "I don't know what he wants."

"Yes you do." Clara moved into the office, settled herself on the battered sofa we kept for clients. "He wants you to see where he lives. Who he is outside the M.O.P. uniform."

"That's not consultation."

"No. It's not." She smiled gently. "Which is why you're going to go."

I wanted to argue. Professional relationships should stay professional. I had work to do, cases pending, clients who needed help more than I needed to waste an afternoon drinking tea in some aristocratic estate.

But I folded the invitation carefully and slipped it into my desk drawer.

"Fine. I'll go."

Thursday arrived too quickly.

I spent the morning attempting to work but mostly rearranging papers and reorganizing files Pip had already organised. Clara finally took pity on me around noon.

"Go upstairs and change. You can't visit Highgate looking like you just finished a contract negotiation."

"I did just finish a contract negotiation."

"Then wash the ink off your hands and put on something that doesn't have tea stains." She shooed me toward the door. "I left the green dress on your bed. The one that makes you look formidable instead of exhausted."

The dress was indeed on my bed, along with stockings without runs and shoes that weren't scuffed to death. Clara had clearly been planning this.

I changed with the quiet anxiety of someone preparing for a test they hadn't studied for. The green wool fit well—Clara knew my measurements better than I did—and the colour brought out something in my complexion that made me look less like I'd been sleeping in my office. Which I had been, but that was beside the point.

The car arrived at precisely two o'clock. Black, official, driven by a uniformed man who opened my door without comment. I slid into the back seat and watched London pass through tinted windows, familiar streets giving way to progressively greener suburbs as we headed north toward Highgate.

Ashwood Manor announced itself through the trees before the gates came into view—glimpses of grey stone and Georgian symmetry visible through autumn-bare branches. The drive wound through grounds that had clearly been maintained for centuries, ancient oaks standing sentinel along the gravel path.

The house itself was exactly what I'd expected and nothing like what I'd imagined. Grand without being ostentatious. Old money architecture that whispered rather than shouted. Three stories of grey stone and perfectly proportioned windows, ivy climbing the eastern wall in careful cultivation.

Frost waited at the front entrance.

He wore civilian clothes—a simple grey wool suit without the M.O.P. insignia, waistcoat buttons gleaming silver. His posture was the same rigid precision I'd grown accustomed to, but something in his expression had softened. Home territory, perhaps. Or something else.

"Miss Blackwell." He descended the steps to meet me as the driver opened my door. "Thank you for coming."

"Your invitation was very formal. I wasn't sure if I should bring case files."

"No case files today." He offered his arm—the gesture automatic, bred into him through generations of aristocratic training. "I thought you might appreciate seeing where the Void seal is maintained. Given everything that happened."

I placed my hand on his sleeve. The contact felt different here than it had in the Obsidian Hall—less anchor, more invitation.

"Lead the way, Inspector."

Ashwood Manor was older than it looked.

The Georgian facade, Frost explained as we walked through corridors lined with family portraits, had been added in the eighteenth century to make the original structure more fashionable. Beneath the elegant plasterwork and wood paneling lay medieval stone, and beneath that, foundations that predated the Norman Conquest.

"My family has maintained this property since the Void seal was first established," he said, guiding me down a staircase that grew progressively older as we descended. Georgian gave way to Tudor, Tudor to something rougher and more ancient. "The responsibility passes through blood. When my father died, it came to me."

"How old were you?"

"Nineteen."

The same age I'd been when Grimsby took me on as an apprentice. When my father's contract had finally finished destroying what remained of our family.

"That's young to carry something like this."

"It was necessary." His voice held no self-pity, only statement of fact. "The seal cannot be unmaintained. If it fails, the Void consumes everything within a mile radius. Thousands of lives. The responsibility doesn't wait for convenient timing."

We reached a door that looked older than anything I'd seen in London—iron-banded oak, covered in sigils that made my eyes water when I tried to focus on them. Frost pressed his scarred palm against a central plate, and the door swung open without sound.

The chamber beyond was vast.

Stone walls curved upward into darkness, the space feeling more like a natural cavern than constructed room. At the center, a circular pattern had been carved into the floor—concentric rings of symbols surrounding a depression that pulsed with faint, cold light.

The Void seal.

Even without Thread Sight, I could feel it. A wrongness at the edge of perception, like standing near a cliff edge in the dark. The knowledge that one step in the wrong direction meant falling into something that had no bottom.

"This is what you protect," I said quietly.

"This is what my family has always protected." Frost moved to stand beside the seal, his posture shifting into something I recognised—the same stance he took when checking his pocket watch. Ritual. Anchoring. "The Void exists in the spaces between dimensions. It presses against reality constantly, seeking entry points. This seal is one of seven in Britain that prevent catastrophic breach."

"And your watch monitors it."

"The watch is bound to the seal's integrity. When the mechanism stutters, the wards are weakening. When it stops..." He didn't need to finish. "I feel it constantly. A pressure at the back of my mind. The awareness of what waits on the other side."

I thought about the controlled precision he maintained at all times. The rigid formality. The way he kept everyone at careful distance.

"That's why you can't afford emotional instability."

"Strong emotions create fluctuations in my magical signature. Those fluctuations can affect the seal's integrity." He met my eyes directly. "I learned very young to maintain control. The alternative was unacceptable."

The weight of what he carried settled over me—not just duty, but constant vigilance. Never being able to fully relax. Never being able to let his guard down without risking catastrophe.

"You came for Clara anyway," I said. "You left this, knowing what it might cost."

"I made arrangements. Augusta maintained the seal while I was absent." His jaw tightened. "But yes. I chose to come."

"Why?"

The question hung between us in the seal chamber's cold air.

Frost was quiet for a long moment. When he spoke, his voice had lost some of its formal distance.

"Because you asked me to choose. Between duty and..." He stopped. Started again. "I have spent my entire adult life believing that duty must come first. That personal connections are dangerous because they create divided loyalties. That the only way to protect what matters is to hold everyone at arm's length."

He turned to face me fully.

"You challenged that belief. You built something worth protecting—Clara, Pip, your practise, your clients—without sacrificing your principles. You proved that connection doesn't have to mean compromise."

"I've compromised plenty."

"Not on the things that matter." His pale grey eyes held mine. "I want to learn how you do that. How you care without breaking. How you fight without losing yourself."

The admission cost him something. I could see it in the tension around his mouth, the careful stillness of his hands.

"Is that what this consultation is about?" I asked. "Learning?"

"This consultation is about offering you resources. M.O.P. support for your practise. Access to case files and investigative authority when you need it. A formal partnership that gives you protection without compromising your independence."

"And unofficially?"

Frost's mouth curved—not quite a smile, but closer than I'd ever seen. "Unofficially, I'm asking if you'd be willing to continue working with me. Not because the Council requires it. Because I find your company... valuable."

"Valuable."

"It's the most accurate word I can identify." The almost-smile deepened slightly. "My vocabulary for personal connection is admittedly limited."

I thought about the past weeks. The warehouse and the Warrens. The Border Realm and the chapel. Standing in the Obsidian Hall watching Clara disappear through a portal, and Frost choosing to stay before duty finally pulled him away. His testimony at the Tribunal, accepting censure without complaint.

"I accept your offer," I said. "The official partnership. M.O.P. resources when needed, consultant status maintained."

"And the unofficial component?"

"I'm still evaluating."

His expression flickered—disappointment, quickly controlled.

"However," I continued, "I'm open to further consultation. Perhaps dinner, at some point. Somewhere that isn't a supernatural crime scene or an ancient seal chamber."

The almost-smile returned. "I believe that can be arranged."

We emerged from the seal chamber into afternoon light that felt impossibly bright after the underground darkness.

Frost led me through the manor's public rooms—library, drawing room, a conservatory filled with plants that shouldn't have survived English winters. He narrated each space with the practised efficiency of someone accustomed to giving tours but not accustomed to caring whether the guest was impressed.

I wasn't impressed. I was paying attention, which was different.

"Can I ask you something?" I said, as we passed through a sitting room whose curtains hadn't been opened in what looked like months.

"Of course."

"Augusta. At the Tribunal—she argued for leniency. She sent me the gown for the Obsidian Hall. She warned me about the conservative faction afterward." I paused, choosing words carefully. "But she also fought reforms for years. Delayed investigation. Protected the same procedural gaps that enabled Vane. I don't understand her."

Frost was quiet for several steps. When he spoke, his voice held something I hadn't heard before—the careful tenderness of someone discussing a person they loved despite everything.

"Augusta was fifteen when her family's estates were nearly destroyed by a reformist faction that moved too quickly. The magical infrastructure collapsed. Three people died. She spent the next sixty years ensuring stability above all else—not because she didn't see the injustice, but because she'd watched what happened when change outpaced the system's capacity to absorb it."

"That doesn't excuse enabling predators."

"No. It doesn't." He met my eyes. "But it explains why she moves slowly. Why she tests every crack before widening it. She's not protecting the powerful because she admires them. She's managing a controlled demolition of a building she knows is rotten, terrified that moving too fast will bring it down on the people still living inside."

"And the gown? The etiquette notes?"

"Augusta never acts without calculation. But she's also capable of genuine concern, expressed through institutional channels because those are the only ones she trusts." His mouth twitched. "She sent the gown because she didn't want you to be dismissed for wearing the wrong thing. That's as close to affection as she allows herself."

I thought about that—about a woman who'd spent decades holding a collapsing system together through sheer political will, watching it fail the people it was supposed to protect, unable to tear it down faster without risking worse.

"I still don't like her."

"You don't have to. You just have to understand what she's doing and why."

We walked on in comfortable silence.

The library held three centuries of accumulated knowledge, shelved floor to ceiling in dark oak. The drawing room was elegant but unused—dust covers on half the furniture, mage-lights dimmed to conservation levels. A house maintained but not lived in. A man who kept the grounds and the facade and the ancient foundations in perfect order, and occupied perhaps four rooms.

We ascended the main staircase toward the first floor, Georgian plasterwork returning around us like a familiar coat pulled over older bones. Family portraits lined the wall at regular intervals, each one formal, unsmiling, bearing the rigidity of people who understood that duty was not a choice but a condition of birth.

I stopped on the landing.

The portrait hung between two windows where the afternoon light caught it fully—a deliberate placement, designed to illuminate rather than merely display. A girl of perhaps thirteen or fourteen, painted in spring light, dark hair falling past her shoulders. She wore a simple blue dress and sat in what I recognised as Ashwood's gardens, the background blooming with early flowers.

Her eyes were grey. Frost's grey. The same pale clarity, the same directness of gaze, but without the careful distance he maintained. Her expression held something his did not—openness. Warmth. The uncomplicated confidence of someone who had not yet learned what the world could take.

"Your sister," I said.

Frost had continued several steps past me before realizing I'd stopped. He turned back, and I watched the shutters come down—the instinctive closing of something that lived too close to the surface.

"Eleanor." He said the name the way one handles old glass—carefully, knowing it could cut. "She was fourteen when that was painted. The last spring."

The last spring. Two words that contained an entire catastrophe.

I looked at the portrait again. At the gardens rendered in careful detail behind her—green and gold and alive in a way that contrasted sharply with the cold radiating from the man standing three steps above me.

"You don't have to tell me," I said.

"No." He descended to stand beside me on the landing, close enough that I could feel the chill that lived beneath his skin. "But I find that I want to. Which is... unusual."

He was quiet for a long moment, studying the portrait with an expression I couldn't fully read—grief, yes, but older than fresh. Grief that had been lived with long enough to become architecture. Something the rest of his life had been built around.

"The seal requires a keeper," he said. "You understand that now—you've felt it. The pressure, the awareness. Maintaining the barrier between reality and the Void is not passive. It demands constant attention. Constant expenditure of magical energy. And over years, over decades, it takes a physical toll."

"The cold."

"The cold." He held up his scarred hand, turning it slowly in the afternoon light. "The Void is absence. The absence of warmth, of light, of matter. When a keeper binds to the seal, they become the conduit through which that absence is... managed. Channeled. Contained. But containment has a cost. The cold bleeds through. Slowly, over years. My grandfather lived to seventy but couldn't feel his hands past sixty. My father..." He paused. "My father began losing warmth at forty-two."

I thought of the ice that formed along Frost's forearms when he used his power. The frost burns on his palms after the warehouse threshold collapsed. Not just magic. Inheritance.

"Your father was the keeper before you."

"For twenty-three years. He managed it well—the decline was gradual, controlled. He maintained function. But by the winter I turned sixteen, the deterioration had accelerated. He couldn't sustain the seal's full integrity for more than a few hours at a time. Augusta supplemented when she could, but she doesn't carry the bloodline bond. Her support was temporary. Insufficient."

He turned from the portrait and walked to the window at the landing's far end. I followed, giving him the physical space the story seemed to require.

"The seal fluctuates," he continued, looking out over grounds that held the stripped dignity of late autumn. "Small pulses of instability that the keeper absorbs. Usually harmless—a moment of cold, a tremor in the watch mechanism. But when my father's control slipped during a particularly severe fluctuation, the pulse wasn't small. It passed through the east wing of the house."

He stopped. His hand found his pocket watch through his waistcoat—not opening it, just pressing his palm against its shape. Anchoring.

"Eleanor's room was in the east wing."

The portrait's spring light felt very far away.

"A Void pulse doesn't kill immediately," Frost said. His voice had gone flat—not cold, but controlled with a precision that told me how much it cost him to maintain. "It strips warmth. Not temperature—warmth. The body's ability to generate and sustain heat. The mundane doctors called it hypothermia, but no amount of blankets or fires could reverse it because the cold wasn't coming from outside. It had been placed inside her, in the space where warmth should have lived."

"How long?"

"Three months." He said it the way one states a distance—factual, measured. "She was lucid for most of it. Aware of what was happening. Our father managed to reseal the breach, but the effort destroyed what remained of his reserves. He died six weeks after the pulse. Eleanor lived another seven weeks beyond that."

Seven weeks. A fourteen-year-old girl, growing colder by degrees in a house already losing its keeper, while her sixteen-year-old brother watched and could do nothing.

"She died in May," he said quietly. "The gardens were blooming. Exactly as they are in that painting. She could see them from her window but couldn't feel the sun through the glass."

I didn't speak. Some things required silence the way wounds required air—not because it healed, but because covering them would be worse.

"I was nineteen when I bound myself to the seal," Frost continued. "Augusta argued against it—said I was too young, that we should find another family to assume the duty, that the cost was too high. But there was no other family with the bloodline affinity, and the seal cannot wait for institutional deliberation. It was necessary."

He turned from the window and met my eyes.

"And I swore that what happened to Eleanor would never happen again. Not to anyone within my protection. Not while I held the seal. The control, the distance, the—" He gestured at himself, a rare unguarded movement that encompassed everything. The formality. The precision. The cold that lived in him. "All of it serves the same purpose. Ensuring that I never lose focus long enough for the Void to take someone else."

I understood, then—not just the facts but the architecture of the man standing in front of me. Every rigid habit, every careful distance, every compulsive check of the pocket watch. Not merely duty. Penance. A sixteen-year-old boy who couldn't save his sister, building a life designed to ensure he never failed anyone again.

And then Clara had been taken. And he had left the seal—the thing he'd built his entire existence around protecting—and walked into the Border Realm because I'd asked him to. Because he'd decided that holding the line wasn't enough if the people behind it were dying.

"The night you came for Clara," I said slowly. "When you left the seal with Augusta and joined us in the kitchen. You weren't just risking the seal's stability."

"No."

"You were risking what happened to Eleanor happening to someone else. To everyone within a mile of this house."

"Yes."

"And you came anyway."

His jaw tightened. "I have spent thirteen years ensuring that no one within my protection suffers what Eleanor suffered. Perfect control. Perfect vigilance. No connections deep enough to compromise that vigilance." He paused. "And then I watched Julian Vane take Clara through a portal, and I understood with absolute clarity that perfect vigilance means nothing if I am perfectly vigilant over a world I have allowed to become unbearable."

The landing held us in afternoon light—the portrait of a girl who had died of cold on one wall, her brother who carried that cold in his blood standing at the window. Between them, the distance of thirteen years and a grief that had become the foundation for everything.

I crossed the landing and stood beside him at the window. Close enough to feel the chill that radiated from his skin. Close enough that my shoulder nearly touched his.

"She looks like you," I said. "The eyes."

"She had my mother's temperament. Warmer than mine, in every sense." The almost-smile appeared—fragile, private. "She would have liked you, I think. She had no patience for formality and very strong opinions about people who used institutional authority to avoid genuine connection."

"She sounds formidable."

"She was fourteen. She would have been formidable, given time." He looked at the portrait one final time, then turned away with the deliberate finality of someone closing a door they'd held open longer than intended. "Come. There's tea, and I believe you haven't eaten since breakfast. You have an expression of someone running on principle rather than sustenance."

"You've learned to identify that expression?"

"You wear it frequently."

I allowed myself to be led away from the landing, away from Eleanor's portrait and the story it contained. But I carried the weight of it with me—the knowledge of what the cold in him meant, what it cost, what he had chosen to risk for Clara and, by extension, for me.

The sitting room waited at the end of the corridor, warm and small by the manor's standards, with tea laid out on a low table. Clara would have approved of the spread: proper china, small sandwiches, scones with clotted cream.

"Your staff anticipated this," I observed.

"I may have suggested that refreshments would be appropriate." He gestured toward a chair. "Please."

We sat across from each other in comfortable silence while I poured tea—he took his without sugar, which didn't surprise me—and worked through the sandwiches with more appetite than I'd felt in days.

"The reforms are being drafted," Frost said eventually. "Lord Ashford is leading the committee. The mandatory Scribe review provisions should be implemented within three months."

"Watered down from what he originally proposed."

"But meaningful nonetheless. The soul-equity threshold requirements alone will prevent the worst forms of extraction." He set down his teacup. "It's not enough. But it's a foundation."

"That's all any of it ever is. Foundations. We build what we can and hope the next generation builds higher."

Frost nodded slowly. "My father said something similar, before he died. That each generation's duty is to leave the world slightly less broken than they found it."

"Did he succeed?"

"I believe so. The question is whether I will."

I thought about Grimsby. About his research, his dedication, his murder. About the work I'd continued in his absence, the clients I'd helped, the reforms that might now actually happen.

"You're already succeeding," I said. "You just can't see it yet because you're too close."

Something shifted in his expression—a crack in the careful control, quickly repaired but visible for an instant. Gratitude, perhaps. Or something more complicated.

"Thank you, Miss Blackwell."

"Imogen." The correction came out before I could stop it. "If we're going to be unofficial colleagues, you should probably use my name."

"Imogen." He tested the word carefully, as if learning a new language. "Then you should call me Nathaniel. When we're not in professional settings."

"Nathaniel." It felt strange on my tongue—too intimate for someone I'd known primarily through crime scenes and courtrooms. But not unpleasant.

The afternoon light slanted through the windows, turning the sitting room golden. For a moment, neither of us spoke.

Then Frost—Nathaniel—checked his pocket watch. The gesture was automatic, reflexive, but he caught himself doing it and smiled ruefully.

"Old habits."

"The seal is stable?"

"Completely. But the monitoring never stops." He closed the watch and returned it to his waistcoat. "I should arrange your return to London. Unless you'd prefer to stay for dinner?"

The invitation was carefully neutral, offering without pressuring. I appreciated the delicacy of it—the acknowledgment that whatever was developing between us needed to unfold slowly, without forcing.

"Another time," I said. "Clara will worry if I'm gone too long. And I have a new client consultation scheduled for tomorrow morning."

"The predatory marriage case? Sarah Mitchell?"

"You've been monitoring my case intake?"

"I've been monitoring potential threats to my consultant." His tone was dry. "Professional interest only."

"Of course."

We both knew it wasn't only professional. But some things didn't need to be said aloud.

The drive back to London felt shorter than the journey out.

I watched the suburbs give way to city streets, grey stone and glass replacing green hedgerows, and thought about foundations. About what we build and what we inherit. About the weight of duty and the possibility of something more.

The car deposited me outside my office as evening fell. The kebab shop was doing brisk business, familiar smells drifting up to where I stood on the pavement.

Clara was waiting in the doorway.

"Well?" She grabbed my arm and pulled me inside before I could answer. "How was it? What did he want? Did anything happen?"

"It was fine. He offered me official M.O.P. partnership. I accepted."

"And?"

"And nothing." I hung up my coat, moved toward my desk. "It was a professional consultation."

Clara's expression suggested she didn't believe me for a moment, but she let it go. "There's tea in the pot. And Pip finished organizing the Mitchell files for tomorrow."

"Thank you."

I settled into my chair, pulled the Mitchell case notes toward me. Predatory marriage contract, debt-binding clauses, a family trying to claim an estate through technicalities. Familiar territory. The kind of work I'd been doing for years, would continue doing for years to come.

But something had shifted. The work felt less like holding back a tide and more like building a foundation.

Pip emerged from his filing cabinet, climbing onto the desk with a stack of precedent notes. "The 1847 ruling is relevant, as I suspected. Also the 1893 reforms and the Whitmore decision. I've flagged the key passages."

"Thank you, Pip."

He paused, studying my face with amber eyes that saw more than they should. "The consultation went well, I take it?"

"It went... productively."

"Hmm." He settled onto his cushion, arranging the notes within easy reach. "Miss Blackwell, I've worked for you for three years. I know what productive looks like on you. This is something else."

"It's complicated."

"Most valuable things are." He picked up a pen nearly as tall as himself and began making notations. "For what it's worth, Lord Frost is a reasonable choice. Politically advantageous, personally compatible, and unlikely to require excessive emotional maintenance."

"That's very romantic of you, Pip."

"Romance is inefficient. Practical partnership is sustainable." But his ears twitched in what might have been amusement. "Though I suppose some inefficiency can be tolerated, in moderation."

Clara brought tea and settled onto the sofa with her own cup. The flat filled with the sounds of evening—traffic below, pipes clanking, the scratch of Pip's pen and the rustle of paper.

Normal. Ordinary. The life I'd built from determination and spite and the belief that someone had to fight for the people the system forgot.

"I was thinking," Clara said quietly. "About the office."

I looked up from the Mitchell files. "What about it?"

"The sign on the door. It still says 'Blackwell, Scribe and Solicitor.'" She set down her teacup. "Maybe it's time for an update."

"What kind of update?"

Clara met my eyes. "Blackwell and Vance. If you'll have me as a partner instead of just an assistant."

The offer caught me off guard. Clara had been helping with my practise for two years, but always in support roles—organizing files, managing clients, keeping the office running while I buried myself in contract work. A partnership was something different. Something permanent.

"You'd want that?" I asked. "After everything?"

"Because of everything." She pulled her cardigan tighter around herself—the nervous gesture I'd come to recognise. "I spent years being someone's victim. His wife, then his widow, then the target of another predator. I'm tired of being defined by what was done to me."

Her voice strengthened as she continued.

"I want to help other people avoid what happened to me. I want to use what I learned—what I survived—to protect people who don't know they need protecting yet. And I want to do it here, with you, building something that matters."

I thought about the case files stacked on my desk. The phone calls that would keep coming. The work that never ended because the system kept creating new victims faster than anyone could help them.

"I can't pay you what you'd be worth," I said.

"I know."

"The work is exhausting and heartbreaking and most of the time we lose."

"I know that too."

"And sometimes clients pay us in vegetables instead of money."

Clara laughed—the first real laugh I'd heard from her since before the Obsidian Hall. "I'll manage."

I stood, crossed to where she sat, and pulled her into a hug.

"Blackwell and Vance it is, then."

She hugged me back fiercely. "Thank you. For everything. For coming for me, for believing in me, for—"

"You don't have to thank me."

"I know. But I want to." She pulled back, wiping her eyes. "Now. About that sign. I know a painter who owes me a favour..."

The new sign went up three days later.

BLACKWELL & VANCE Contract Law & Working-Class Advocacy Consultations by Appointment

The painter had done good work—gold letters on dark green, professional without being ostentatious. It looked like what it was: a small practise run by people who cared more about their clients than their profit margins.

Pip emerged from the filing cabinet with a small card pinched between his paws—heavy cream stock, the Registry's official watermark visible in the corner.

"I've taken the liberty of amending your professional designation," he announced. "The Registry now lists: *Blackwell, I.—Scribe, Solicitor, and Barrister.* It required a larger card."

"I haven't earned that title. There are examinations. Fees. The Inns of Court—"

"You argued before the High Council in a salt circle and won." Pip set the card on my desk with ceremonial precision. "If that doesn't qualify as advocacy certification, then the entire examination system is even more fraudulent than your Null-Ink signatures."

I picked up the card. The ink was fresh, the letters precise in Pip's meticulous hand.

Barrister.

I hadn't earned it the proper way—hadn't paid the fees or sat the examinations or cultivated the right connections. I'd earned it by standing in a courtroom I was never supposed to enter and arguing so effectively that the system had to acknowledge me whether it wanted to or not.

The title of the book I hadn't written yet. The name for what I'd become.

I set the card beside the Null-Ink pen on my desk and went back to work.

I stood on the pavement below, watching morning light catch the fresh paint, and felt something settle in my chest. Not peace, exactly. The work was still overwhelming, the system still broken, the phone still ringing with new cases every day.

But foundation. That's what this was. Something to build on.

Pip appeared at the window above, his small face pressed against the glass. He gave a thumbs up—the gesture incongruously human from someone so distinctly not—then disappeared back into the office.

Clara joined me on the pavement, two cups of tea in hand. She passed one over without comment, and we stood together looking up at our names.

"It's real now," she said quietly.

"It was always real. This just makes it official."

"Official matters." She sipped her tea. "Contracts and all that."

I thought about contracts. About the ones that bound and the ones that freed. About the weight of obligation and the possibility of choice.

"We should get to work," I said. "Sarah Mitchell's consultation is in an hour."

"I've got the files ready. Pip's already pulled the precedents."

We climbed the stairs together, entering the office that was now officially ours. The familiar mess of papers and books and legal documents. Pip's meticulously organised filing system. The battered sofa and the window overlooking the street.

Home.

The phone rang.

I crossed to my desk and picked up the receiver.

"Blackwell and Vance, how may I help you?"

A woman's voice, uncertain and afraid. "I... I heard about what you did. The Tribunal. The reforms. I have a problem with a contract my husband signed, and I don't know who else to call..."

I pulled a notepad toward me, uncapped my pen.

"Tell me about the contract. Start from the beginning."

While she talked, I took notes. Clara brought fresh tea. Pip began pulling relevant files.

Outside, London continued its double existence—mundane and magical, overlapping and hidden. Somewhere in that layered city, people were signing contracts that would destroy them. Somewhere, predators were preparing new schemes. Somewhere, the system was failing people who trusted it to protect them.

We couldn't fix all of it. Couldn't save everyone. Couldn't remake the world into something fair and just through sheer stubbornness.

But we could answer the phone. Take the cases. Fight the battles that others wouldn't fight.

One client at a time. One contract at a time. One small victory at a time.

The work continued.

And we would continue with it.

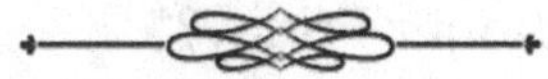

Three weeks later

The evening post brought two items of interest.

The first was a formal notice from the High Council: the compromise reforms had been drafted and would take effect at the start of the new year. Mandatory Scribe review for contracts exceeding soul-equity thresholds. standardised dissolution clauses in marriage agreements. Increased penalties for documented fraud.

Insufficient. But meaningful.

The second was a handwritten note on cream-coloured paper, frost crystal seal on the envelope.

Imogen,

The investigation into the Severing Shears' provenance continues, though official channels remain closed. I have identified three potential sources for artifacts of that era. Would you be available Friday evening to review the findings? Dinner at eight, location of your choosing.

Nathaniel

I read the note twice, then set it beside my tea.

Clara noticed immediately. "Another consultation?"

"Something like that."

"Mm-hmm." Her tone suggested she knew exactly what kind of consultation this was. "Should I not expect you for dinner Friday?"

"I'll be late."

"Take your time." She returned to her filing, but I caught her smile. "Some consultations are worth being thorough about."

I didn't dignify that with a response. Instead, I pulled fresh paper from my drawer and began composing a reply.

Nathaniel,

Friday at eight is acceptable. There's a restaurant in Clerkenwell that serves adequate food and asks no questions about unusual dinner conversation topics. I'll send the address.

Regarding the Shears—whoever provided them to Vane had access to artifacts that supposedly don't exist. That suggests either very old money or very new connections to people who collect dangerous things. The Council's refusal to investigate officially is suspicious. Someone on that bench knows more than they're admitting.

Something else has been troubling me. You told me the seal destabilised thirteen years ago—that the fluctuation that reached Eleanor was a consequence of your father's declining control. But Grimsby's notes document coordinated magical interference beginning roughly fifteen years ago. Two years before your father's health failed. I am not suggesting a connection. I am noting a coincidence, and I have never believed in coincidence. Neither, as you once told me, do you.

We should discuss this further. Among other things.

Imogen

I sealed the letter, addressed it to Ashwood Manor, and set it aside for the morning post.

Outside, London settled into evening. Streetlights flickered on. The kebab shop below began its dinner rush.

Somewhere in the city, someone was holding a pair of ancient shears that could sever any binding. Someone had given Julian Vane the tools to murder, and that someone was still free. The case was officially closed, but the mystery remained.

I would find the answer. We would find it—Frost and I, working the edges of what was permitted, pushing against the boundaries of what was possible.

The system was broken. The law enabled exploitation. Power protected predators.

The system hadn't been fixed. One tribunal and a handful of reforms didn't undo centuries of engineered inequality. But something had shifted—a crack in the foundation that couldn't be plastered over. The law was still a weapon. The question was no longer whether it could be wielded differently, but who would be holding it next.

I picked up my pen and returned to the Mitchell case notes.

The work continued. And tomorrow, there would be more.

www.ingramcontent.com/pod-product-compliance
Lightning Source LLC
LaVergne TN
LVHW030917080826
845145LV00013B/2935